# THE VALKYRIE MANDATE

ROBERT VAUGHAN

**WOLFPACK**
**PUBLISHING**
— EST 2013 —

**The Valkyrie Mandate**
Paperback Edition
© Copyright 2021(as revised) Robert Vaughan

Wolfpack Publishing
5130 S. Fort Apache Rd. 215-380
Las Vegas, NV 89148

wolfpackpublishing.com

Paperback ISBN 978-1-63977-089-2

# THE VALKYRIE MANDATE

# THE VALKYRIE MANDATE

# NOTE FROM THE AUTHOR OF THE VALKYRIE MANDATE

I would like to submit for your reading enjoyment, my book *The Valkyrie Mandate*. Previously published, this edition has been revised and updated. I removed some material from the original and I have added to the narrative for a smoother transition.

It is my belief that one can learn more history from a novel written in accurate detail, than from a non-fiction history tome. My reasoning for this is because in a novel, the reader, through the characters, becomes an actual part of the events. Many historians believe that the assassination of Ngo Dinh Diem was the catalyst to our increased participation in the Vietnam War, and my novel *The Valkyrie Mandate* covers that incident in heavily researched, and extremely accurate detail.

During my last tour in Vietnam one of the Vietnamese who worked for me, was a man named Jung Il Mot. While waiting for a train to pass on Railroad Crossing Number Six of Tru Minh Young Street, Mot said, "This is where it happened."

When I asked where what happened, he said "This is

where President Diem was killed." He then showed me a handkerchief with the brown stains of Diem's blood.

As it turned out, Mot had been a private, who was present in the armored personnel carrier in which Diem and his brother, Nhu, were assassinated by Major Nguyễn Văn Nhung, (who himself was killed a few days later).

Becoming interested in the subject, I began with Mot's eye-witness account of the actual killings. But I wanted to know what led up to it, I wanted facts on the coup itself, so I started my research in great detail by going through the archives of the *Saigon Post*, which was an English language newspaper. From there I visited with Father Guimet at St. Francis Xavier Church in Cholon, because Father Guimet is the one who took Diem and Nhu's last confession.

I continued my research after returning to the States, interviewing Father DePaul, who was a long-time personal friend of Diem's. Then, while working in the office of Congressman Tommy Downing of Virginia, I had access to State and Defense Department papers, detailing U.S. involvement in the coup. During the Watergate Hearings, these papers were burned by FBI Chief, L. Patrick Gray.

I also contacted Madam Nhu to ask for an interview, but she wanted

$25,000 before she would talk to me, so I passed on that.

I hope you enjoy the book.

Robert Vaughan

*Saigon, Vietnam –August, 1963:*

*"BUN MAE! BUN MAE!"*

Bare feet whispers softly on ground still damp with the morning dew.

*"Bun mae, Bun mae!"* The haunting call hangs in the air and penetrates the walls of the small houses.

In Saigon, there is scarcely enough time in one day for the poor people to make a living. So, long before the sun rises, they are out working, trying to stretch the hours to meet their needs.

Old women, their teeth and gums blackened with betel nut, shuffle through the narrow, twisting, back alleys. They pick their way through the garbage and sewage, stoically attending to their profession, be it trading, begging, or selling.

The queen of the morning is clearly the bread woman. Of all the city smells the aroma of her hot bread, *bun mae,* wrapped in newspaper, is the richest. Small groups of children, the poorest of the poor, follow her.

They fight over the occasional bread crumbs that spill from her baskets and beg for bread from her customers. Her singing cry *"Bun mae!"* is heard in hundreds of homes, where for a brief moment the whole family is together. They huddle comfortably around the small cooking fire, and her chant assures them that their world has not disappeared during the night.

Not all Saigon is awake. Some of the houses along the twisting streets are occupied by prostitutes and mistresses of the soldiers. They are still in bed, sleeping on silk sheets and satin pillows. Although from the outside their houses look the same as the others, inside there are many luxuries to reflect the money the girls make. Most of the girls are sleeping alone, their last customers long gone, but some are still sharing their beds, and the bread woman's cry recalls something from their childhood. They stir slightly, then, feeling a man in bed with them, smile at their good fortune, throw a leg over him to snuggle up closer, and drift back into a comfortable sleep.

The cyclos appear then. Small, three-wheeled motor bikes, with a passenger seat in front and a sputtering, popping motor in the rear. They dart in and out of the alleys and back streets and zip up and down Cong Ly and Tru Minh Ky looking for riders. The cyclos trail clouds of noxious exhaust smoke, which by late afternoon will lie over the city in a thick blue fog. By sunrise all the streets are covered with them, not only the busy thoroughfares but the quieter streets as well, including the streets around the presidential palace.

Barbed-wire barricades and sandbag-invested walls keep the traffic a full block away from President Ngo Dinh Diem's place of residence. The guards are young men in crisp khakis, with red sashes and shining chrome helmets. They stand around in small booths listening to transistor radios and eating their breakfast bowl of soup. To the Americans—and there are some sixteen thousand in Vietnam by now—the lax posture of the guards seems almost shocking.

On this particular Tuesday morning, August 20, 1963, the guards seemed particularly lax. Many had left their weapons in the guard booths and had spread out a bamboo mat for a community breakfast. They held the rice bowls against their chins, snapping their chopsticks open and shut, and exchanging gossip and jokes while they ate. They didn't see the Lambretta "scooterwagon" approach the main barricade.

Five Buddhist monks got out and sat cross-legged before the barricade, then a sixth poured gasoline over them. All five monks touched matches to themselves, and only when the flames had completely enveloped them did one of the guards notice and let out a yell.

The guards ran to the monks but were unable to do anything but stand with the rapidly gathering crowd and watch as the monks sat there, being quietly consumed by fire. Cyclos, taxis, and chauffeur-driven Mercedes screeched to a halt as all classes of Vietnamese were drawn to the scene of horror by the morbid fascination of sudden death.

Suddenly a series of shots rang out from the palace grounds, and the guards, as if realizing their duty for the first time, started up the long driveway on the run. There were a few more shots, then an explosion, loud, and with a heavy shock wave.

When the guards reached the palace, they saw the front door blasted off its hinges. The same Lambretta that had just let off the monks was twisted and smoking. It had obviously been loaded with explosives and driven into the door in an attempt to breach the palace walls.

Colonel Thric Thi Doung was standing in front of the smoking wreckage, holding a pistol. He was the Commander of the Special Police and one of the men directly responsible for the safety of Diem. He looked up in anger as the officer of the detail on duty, and the guards themselves, came running.

"How can this be?" he exploded. "A guard booth every twenty-five meters and this person drives right up to the front door!"

The officer of the guard bowed and began offering apologies. "We were tricked. Five monks set fire to themselves to create a diversion, and that must be when the assassin got through! Is the President safe?"

"Yes," Colonel Doung answered. "But he cannot thank his palace guard for that. Report to your superior at once. You are relieved!"

The officer of the guard saluted, bowed slightly, then left in disgrace.

"Colonel, the terrorist still lives," one of the men said.

"Bring him to me," Colonel Doung replied, almost spitting the words as he spoke.

The monk was very young. One arm had been almost torn off by the explosion, and he tried futilely to cover the gaping hole with his hand. His saffron robe was soaked red with blood. The loss of so much blood, coupled with his condition of shock, had given his skin a blue tone. He was dragged before Colonel Doung and held up by two guards.

"Whom do you serve?" Colonel Doung asked. "Buddha or Ho Chi Minh?"

The young bonze licked his lips but did not answer.

"What sect sent you?" Colonel Doung asked. He slid

the breach of his pistol back, cocking it. He pointed it at the young man's face.

"Who sent you?" he asked again, very calmly.

The youth still did not answer.

Colonel Doung pulled the trigger, and the heavy 45-caliber bullet crashed into the monk's face, and spattered blood and small slivers of bone on the khaki shirts of the two guards holding him. The impact of the bullet was so severe that it tore the prisoner from the grip of the guards and slammed him back onto the steps, where he lay, looking like a pile of blood-soaked rags.

"Clean this mess up," Colonel Doung ordered as he put his pistol back in his holster.

Colonel Doung pulled out a silk handkerchief and began wiping his hands with it as he walked down the driveway toward the front gate. There was a large crowd when he got there, and he ordered them dispersed.

"I have tried to send them away, but they won't go," one of the guards complained.

"This is how you make them go," Colonel Doung said angrily. He grabbed a Thompson submachine gun from one of the guards and turned to face the crowd.

"Go back, beyond the next barricade!" he shouted.

A few people moved away, but most remained, unable to give up their almost sensual enjoyment over still being alive in the presence of such recent death.

Colonel Doung cocked the gun and then fired a burst over the head of the crowd. The other guards quickly joined him.

"I said go back to the next barricade!"

The crowd started then, slowly at first, but when Colonel Doung fired a second time they ran in a panic, knocking down the slower ones, the old, the crippled, and the very young who stood in their way.

"If they return, shoot to kill," Colonel Doung said to the guards.

"Yes, sir," the guards answered.

Colonel Doung held the submachine gun on his hip and stood over what was left of one of the monks. His body, like that of the other four, was nothing but a blackened chunk. It was totally unrecognizable as ever having been a human being. The chunks of burned flesh were still hot, and small wisps of smoke curled up from them.

"They smell like roast pork," Colonel Doung said. He laughed. "Have we any apples to put in their mouths?" One of the younger guards turned away quickly, then ran over to his guard booth and began to vomit.

"What's this?" Colonel Doung teased. "One of my brave soldiers with a queasy stomach?"

"Colonel Doung," a messenger said, "The President wishes to see you."

Colonel Doung smiled. "I am not surprised." If anyone else had been in Doung's place that morning he might have felt intimidated. He might have approached a meeting with the President, whose life had just been endangered, with a feeling of fear or nervousness; but not Doung. Doung felt elated.

It had been an exciting morning, and waves of ecstasy still washed across Doung as he recalled killing the young monk. His pulse quickened with exhilaration as he passed the steps and saw the soldiers washing away the blood. President Diem was sitting on the edge of his bed in the dingy and untidy room that served as his bedroom. One white suit lay in a heap on a chair, awaiting the laundry, and Diem was putting on another double-breasted, white sharkskin, exactly like the soiled one. A plethora of American men's magazines featuring scantily-clad women lay scattered around.

6

Diem had long ago taken a vow of celibacy, and his penchant for girlie magazines was not widely known. Doung felt it an indication of the President's confidence in him to be allowed into this inner sanctum, where the most intimate secrets were bared.

"Where is my brother?" Diem asked, grunting slightly as he bent over to lace his shoes. "Is he all right?"

"Yes, Excellency," Doung answered. "As is your sister-in-law."

Diem smiled wryly. "I imagine Madam Nhu is talking a great deal."

Doung returned the smile. "She finds much to talk about."

"But little to say," Diem replied. He straightened up, saw an open magazine on the bed, and allowed his eyes to linger, almost hungrily, on the nude blonde in the photo spread.

"The Americans come here and enjoy our women. It would be nice, perhaps, if they would also send some of their women for us to enjoy, would it not?" Doung rasped in a lecherous voice.

"I'm sure I wouldn't know," Diem said sharply. "As you well know, I've taken a vow of celibacy."

Doung felt a stinging embarrassment. He had nearly overstepped his bounds, and his feeling of exhilaration was dimmed somewhat by the blunder.

"Please ask my brother to meet me in the Council Chamber."

"Yes, Mister President," Doung replied, with a slight bow.

Ngo Dinh Nhu, his mouth drawn in a tight line, his eyes flashing anger, tapped his bony fingers against the windowsill as he looked out onto the palace grounds.

"It was not my idea to make concessions in June," he

7

said. "But we made them anyway. And what have we gained?"

"The Americans have threatened to withhold aid if we don't make more concessions," Diem said in almost a whining tone.

"The Americans." Nhu spat derisively. "They are worse than the French." Nhu smiled. "But when their new ambassador, the one who ran for Vice President, arrives, he will be powerless to interfere with us. Plans are already under way, and he will be greeted with a fait accompli. The Buddhist problem will be solved.

"What have you done?" Diem asked.

"Diem, my brother, you are president, and should occupy your time with affairs of state. Leave such matters in the hands of the Can Lao," Nhu suggested.

"Your secret police," Diem said.

"The government's intelligence service," Nhu corrected.

"Loyal to you," Diem said resolutely.

"But of course, Excellency, I am loyal to you," Nhu said smoothly.

As Doung watched the conversation between President Diem and his brother Nhu, it seemed difficult to accept the fact that they were brothers, and that in the division of power, legal power rested with Diem. For Diem, round-faced and chubby, was hesitant and apologetic. Nhu, on the other hand, had no official status whatever other than advisor to his brother. He was skinny, had a prominent Adam's apple and angry piercing eyes. But he was self-assured and made apologies to no one.

Diem plucked at the bridge of his nose with his thumb and forefinger, using the traditional Vietnamese method of trying to cure a headache. "Do as you think best, Nhu. I want no part of it."

"Colonel Doung," Nhu said. "The American advisor to your office, Colonel Barclay, does he know of the plans for tonight?"

"He knows nothing."

"He is one American we must fear. He speaks our language like a native and could easily overhear information. It is so unusual for an American to speak Vietnamese that our people speak freely around them."

"All members of my Special Police know of Colonel Barclay's talent," Doung said. "We have taken precautions. Colonel Barclay suspects nothing."

Doung was wrong. Colonel Barclay, who was at the Special Police headquarters on Le Loi, was suspicious of something. But he didn't know what. Twice that morning he had left his office and walked into the large room where the information-processing department was, and all conversation had stopped. The first time it hadn't registered, but now, when he had come in for a cup of coffee, the interruption in conversation had been so abrupt that it was immediately noticeable.

Colonel Justin Barclay was a big man—six feet four, two-hundred-twenty pounds. He had red hair and a square boxer's face. His forearms, exposed by his rolled-up fatigue shirt sleeves, were covered with freckles and rippling with muscle. He stirred sugar into his coffee and looked out across the room at the working Vietnamese. They were in a flurry of activity under his gaze, filing papers, writing reports, and so forth. Justin returned to his office and to his work. He was senior American advisor to the Special Police. He was unique among American advisors because he not only spoke Vietnamese, he understood; and there is a big difference.

To most of Vietnam the United States is a deaf mute, except on the very formal, high-level diplomatic exchange. Nuances and shades of opinion are never exchanged. But Justin could speak with the lowest peasant or the highest official. He understood perfectly the Oriental thinking patterns and the skillful subtleties with which "yes," "no," and "maybe" may take on many different meanings.

Justin was a member of the ASA, the Army Security Agency. He had first come to Vietnam in 1953 as an American advisor to the French, and had remained. He had a total of ten years there, and it was said of him that if Vietnam were a state in the United States, Justin would be overwhelmingly elected to Congress. He knew hundreds of people in all the surrounding villages, and in honor of him many Vietnamese children had the unlikely name of Barclay, or My Di Wi—"American Captain." To most Vietnamese the title "Captain" fits any military position of great respect.

Justin's phone rang, and he grabbed it on the first ring, grateful for the interruption in his paper work.

"Colonel Barclay, Doung here. We had some distasteful business this morning. Perhaps you heard. Some more monks burned themselves, and attacked the palace."

"Yes," Justin replied. "I heard the news."

"Because of this I will be busy and cannot keep an appointment with my wife. I was to meet her at the Continental Hotel this afternoon. Would you meet her for me? She will be expecting you."

"Yes, of course," Justin said. "Is there anything I can do to help you out down there?"

"It's routine now," Doung said easily. "But it will keep me busy for the entire day."

"I will give Madam Doung your apologies," Justin offered.

Justin had met Madam Doung on a few occasions, but always at some official function. They had spoken only briefly, and always on a very polite and formal level. But pictures of Madam Doung had graced the pages of newspapers and magazines around the world. In her official capacity as wife of one of the most powerful figures in the Saigon government, she was present at many state functions. And because she was an exceptionally beautiful woman, she provided the spark of glamor photographers liked to catch at such affairs.

Across Saigon, in a luxurious old French villa, an exquisitely beautiful woman was giving instructions to her servants. Madam Doung was preparing to go out, and as she moved around, a hint of Shalimar lingered in the air behind her. She stood in her boudoir contemplating the selection of her dress. Several brightly colored *ao dai* lay across her silk-sheeted bed, placed there by the servants, who had then melted discreetly into the shadows of the house, leaving Madam Doung to make her decision.

Le had married Thric Thi Doung because it had been arranged for her by her grandfather. It was a perfectly normal thing for him to do. Le's father had lived in France, and her grandfather was too old to bear the responsibility for a young girl, so when he saw the opportunity to make a good marriage for his granddaughter, he took advantage of it.

Le had never really envisioned any other type of life. At least, not until the Americans began to come to Vietnam and she began to meet the wives and families of the officers assigned to Saigon. Then she read the American magazines and learned their customs. And the custom that appealed most to her was the way the American women had the freedom to choose their own husbands.

Now, because she knew that there were places in the world where she would have been able to resist her marriage, she was bitterly unhappy. She felt as if she were a prisoner, trapped in the body which happened to be born Vietnamese. It was a state of misery that Le believed would be hers for the rest of her life. Divorce was out of the question not only because it was against the law of Vietnam, but also because she knew that she would not be able to deny who and what she was.

Le called to her servants, then walked into a bathroom which was filled with the scent of expensive perfume. She stood beside the bath for an instant, then, when the dressing gown was removed from her shoulders, she stepped into the tub and slid down into the fragrant water.

## 2

TU DO STREET IS A VERY BROAD BOULEVARD THAT RUNS from the river to a square in the heart of Saigon. Each side of the avenue is lined with flowering mimosa and magnolia trees, and the street is divided by a wide ribbon of palms and grass.

Numerous flower stalls are established along this center island. There, the shopkeepers sell cut flowers. They feature all types of floral arrangements, from the traditional Western bouquet style of many varieties to the delicate Oriental *Ikebana*, with the three stems, known as *shuski*, representing heaven, earth, and man.

Tu Do Street is known as the "Street of Flowers," and the natural inclination would be to believe that it is so called because of the many flower stalls along its length. But that isn't the case. The "flowers" in the Street of Flowers are the prostitutes who work the street. It is, by some unique tradition lost in antiquity, the only street in Saigon where the girls themselves appear openly to proposition customers. Throughout the rest of the city, contact must be made through a pimp, a taxi driver, or some other intermediary.

Like the cut flowers for whom they are named, the girls appear in all styles. Some have had cosmetic surgery to build out their noses and make their eyes look round, a drastic step, because it marks them for the rest of their lives as having been an "American whore." Some, despite Madam Nhu's ban on all but conservative Vietnamese dress, wear the latest American styles. But most of them realize that the Vietnamese girls are among the most beautiful in the world, and rather than mask their fragile, graceful beauty, they accent it. They wear *ao dai*, free-flowing dresses in butterfly-bright silk. Their hair, instead of being bobbed and set, hangs luxuriously down their backs.

All up and down the sidewalks on both sides of Tu Do Street blankets are spread out and loaded with goods for sale. The vendors are the last link in a chain of black market and corruption which starts on the docks and at the airports and is so efficient that entire cargoes have disappeared without a trace. The sidewalk vendors take the highest risk and make the least profit. Their risks are high because, in the occasional surges of getting rid of corruption, the government seldom goes deeper than the visible layer, the sidewalk vendors. Smashing them gives an appearance of something being done. There are so many who must get their hands in the pie; therefore, the sidewalk vendors' profits are so low that they are unable to pay the protection money necessary to avoid harassment.

The legitimate businesses in Saigon are a delightful blend of Oriental tradition and culture, and French influence. This is especially true of the hotels and restaurants.

The cuisine at almost any Saigon restaurant is among the finest in the world because the Vietnamese have a natural ability to create culinary art. It was precisely for this reason that Escoffier, regarded by many as the finest chef the world has ever known, chose as his chief pastry baker a Vietnamese named Nguyen Sinh Cung. Although he was an excellent baker and had the finest references and credentials from Escoffier, this particular Vietnamese went on to other things. One of the other things this baker, whose changed his name to Ho Chi Minh, did was to become leader of North Vietnam.

The Continental Hotel is an example of one of the fine blends of culture in the city. It sits on a busy corner in the heart of Saigon, and an open veranda affords customers the luxury of sitting quietly over a drink or a meal while they watch the people of the city pass by. Overhead fans turn briskly, and white-jacketed waiters dart about carrying gin-ton and other cooling drinks balanced on serving trays.

Justin pulled into the no-parking zone in front of the hotel, passed a chain through the steering wheel, and locked it. He was driving a Jeep marked with the colors and signs of the Special Police, so he didn't worry about the no-parking area, even though a policeman stood by. The policeman was dressed in the white uniform of the National Police—"White Mice," the GIs called them. He was not a part of the Special Police, and so shared the national fear and distrust of them, and his attitude showed in his face as he looked at Justin.

Justin had made urgent appeals to Colonel Doung to change the image the people had of the Special Police. He knew that it would always be their nature to be suspicious, and even fearful of them, but their attitude now was far beyond that.

An old man shuffled up to Justin. Long wisps of white hair protruded from his chin to form a beard which waved in the gentle breeze. The man clasped his palms together and dipped his hands several times in a position of groveling respect. He stared at Justin with the eyes of a man who had lived beyond his time and had been turned out by his family, to beg or die.

"Venerable one, it is I who should honor you and the wisdom of your years," Justin said, returning the gesture and then pressing a hundred pastries into the man's hands. The old man was so shocked at hearing Justin speak Vietnamese, that it was several seconds before he realized the enormity of his prize. He grasped it tightly to prevent it from getting away and shuffled quickly over to a sidewalk vendor to buy a bowl of *My ton* soup and the special treat of a bottle of beer.

Justin would have preferred a table right at the entrance, but it was occupied by a man Justin recognized as the Minister of Imports. He was reading a newspaper, and the fat, sausage-like fingers of both his hands were adorned with diamond rings. Rolls of flesh from his thick neck lay in layers across the silk collar of his expensive suit. The conversations being conducted in the Continental were in French, Vietnamese, and Chinese. Justin could not follow the Chinese, but the French and Vietnamese conversations dealt with things as diverse as the price of rubber on the international market to a ballet being performed in Cholon.

No one was talking about the Buddhist suicides, and Justin saw a perfect example of something that he frequently tried to point out to other Americans but was unable to make them grasp. The stratum of society represented by the people with whom Americans normally had contact was totally isolated from the mainstream of the Vietnamese people.

It curled and seeped through the population like an oil slick on water, moving with the current, seemingly a part of the whole but never actually emulsifying.

A taxi pulled to a stop at the curb, and Justin watched as a woman sitting in the shadows of the back seat passed money across to the driver. When she stepped out of the car Justin recognized her as Madam Doung.

Justin watched as she approached the entrance. He guessed her age as under thirty. She had high cheekbones, not prominent but well accented. Even at a distance Justin could see that her eyes sparkled like set jewels and were framed by eyelashes as beautiful as the most delicate lace. Her skin was smooth and gold. Her movements were as graceful as palm fronds stirred by a breeze. Justin believed that he had never seen a more breathtakingly beautiful woman.

Justin met her at the entrance, and when she smiled and offered her hand, he took it. "Madam Doung, it is a pleasure to see you again. I am sorry that I must be a poor substitute for your husband. He has been unavoidably detained by pressing business."

Le laughed, and the laughter fell from her lips like the tinkling of wind chimes. "That is his excuse," she said. "The truth is, he didn't want to meet me. I must go to Phu Coung, a small village not far from here, and visit the orphanage my grandfather started. Doung does not like doing things like this."

"Madam Doung, I would be glad to take you," offered Justin.

"Only if you call me Le, not Madam Doung," Le replied. "In your country, friends, even men and women, address each other by their given names, is this not so?"

"Yes," Justin said. "I am called Justin."

"Then I shall call you Justin," Le said, only the name came out as "Yustin." Because of the accent and the inflection of her voice, the name was almost a caress to the ears when she spoke it, and Justin derived a great deal of pleasure in hearing her say it.

"Would you like a drink before we go?" Justin asked.

"I think not. The children will be looking for me," Le replied.

The drive to Phu Coung was quite pleasant once the river was crossed and the congestion of Saigon was behind them. Highway 13 wound through lush green fields and quiet little villages. Brilliant splashes of color lined the road as flowers grew in profusion.

THE ORPHANAGE WAS BADLY UNDERSTAFFED and overpopulated. Justin looked around the grounds while Le conducted business with the director. As Justin walked around, he became the center of attention of every child in the institution. They laughed and shouted to one another, and pulled at the hair on his arms, amazed to find hair growing in such a place. They were awed by his red hair, and the shape and color of his blue eyes, but mostly by his size. To the children it was as if a giant had come to life from one of their stories.

They spent most of the day there, and drove back to Saigon in the late afternoon.

"I come here two times every week," Le said. "Doung does not like this place. Would you like to bring me more often?"

Justin didn't get a chance to answer. A sudden burst of machine-gun fire smashed through the windshield of the Jeep, exploding the glass in a shower. The bullets slammed into the hood and radiator, and into the front tire, blowing it out with a bang. The Jeep lurched off the side of the road and down a slight embankment, coming to rest on its side. Steam gushed out of the punctured radiator.

Justin had been thrown from the Jeep, and he rolled down the embankment, slamming against rocks, smashing through the brush, which tore at his clothing and scratched his skin. He wound up face down in the bottom of the ditch, with a salty taste in his mouth from the gash he had bitten into his lip. He pulled himself up painfully and took a few seconds to decide that he wasn't hurt. He thought of Le.

"Le, Le, are you all right?" he yelled, running for the Jeep.

"Yes," Le answered, "I think so. What happened?" Suddenly Justin remembered that they had been ambushed and that the attackers might be coming for them. He pulled his pistol and scrambled up to the side of the road. He looked over toward the direction from which the shots were fired and saw two men running back toward a tree line.

They were carrying AK-47 automatic rifles, and Justin had only his pistol. He decided not to shoot at them for fear of disclosing how poorly armed he was, so he holstered his pistol and slid back down the embankment to look at Le.

Le was sitting on the ground beside the Jeep. The bright yellow silk of her ao dai was stained red, and Justin was afraid that she may have been hit in the chest. He looked closely but could see no pumping of blood, nor could he find a puncture in the dress where a bullet may have passed through. Le was being very quiet, and Justin feared that she might be going into shock.

There was a movement behind him and an excited murmur of voices. Justin pulled his gun and turned around quickly.

A handful of Vietnamese, residents of the tiny village of Hoa Ginh, had come to see what was going on. When they saw Justin spin around with a gun in his hand they attempted to scramble back up the embankment and yelled at each other in fright, warning of the Special Police.

Justin suddenly realized that what had frightened them most was the fact that they recognized the Jeep as being a Special Police Jeep.

"Wait," Justin called. "We are not Special Police. Wait!" A few stopped and looked back. "Why did you want to shoot us?" one of them asked.

"I didn't know who you were. I thought you might be the people who did this. This lady is..." Justin suddenly stopped. He was about to tell them who Le was, but he remembered how they had reacted to the sight of the Special Police Jeep. If they knew Le was the wife of the director of the Special Police, they might run again. "This lady is hurt," Justin said. "I need help with her."

"We will take her to my house," one of the Vietnamese said, and a couple of them picked Le up and led Justin into one of the small huts.

The floor of the hut was hard-packed dirt. The roof was of straw, and the sides laced bamboo, plastered with a two-inch-thick layer of hard mud. A bed—no mattress just a frame and a straw mat—a crudely constructed table, a handful of boxes, and the large earthenware crock that held the family supply of rice were the extent of the furnishings. A little girl and a little boy squatted, naked, in a corner, and watched with gleaming, curious eyes as they entered. In his excitement the little boy began to urinate, and the yellow stream passed around his heels and under the wall of the hut unnoticed by anyone present.

Le was placed on the bed.

The hut had filled with the curious, and they spoke quietly and crowded around the bed to look at the "beautiful wounded lady."

Justin knew that he was going to have to look at the wound, but he was a little reluctant to expose Le to the onlookers. Finally he appealed to one of the old women, asking her to move the others away and to help him examine the wound in modesty.

The appeal worked. The woman began yelling at the others, and they left, reluctant to take themselves away from this exciting diversion in their daily routine.

The woman produced a pair of scissors, obviously one of the most treasured possessions in the family, and began cutting away the front of Le's dress.

There was no bullet hole. The blood had come from a couple of small wounds made by slivers of glass, and the old woman removed the slivers and then bathed Le's chest.

Once Justin was reassured that the danger was minimal he stood quietly, watching the old woman work. He handed the first-aid kit he had brought from the Jeep to the old woman, who finished the job nicely.

Justin gave the woman some money, asked her to find something Le could wear, then went back outside to see if he could flag down a ride to Saigon. To his surprise, his Jeep was sitting back on the road. The spare tire had been put on the front, and the Vietnamese had formed a sort of bucket brigade, using tin cans, small cups, gourds, anything that would hold water. They stood in line, each one giving instructions to the other on how to pour water into the radiator. When someone's time came, he would make a big show of demonstrating the correct procedure. More than half the water got on the ground, but eventually the radiator was filled. The holes had been plugged with a raw-gum base, and the Jeep, if not good as new, was at least up to the trip back to Saigon.

A few minutes later, Le emerged from the hut wearing a smock provided by the old woman. Every citizen in Hoa Ginh stood by the Jeep, all proud of their handiwork, not only in fixing the Jeep but in fixing the lady as well. Le and Justin thanked them, then drove away.

Le looked at her smock. "I am wearing the clothes of an old woman," she said. "I must look old."

"You have the clothes of an old woman but the body of a beautiful young woman," Justin said.

When they returned to Saigon, they found the traffic even heavier than usual. That was because of the big Buddhist funeral parade honoring the five monks who had committed suicide. The body of the sixth bonze was still in the hands of the government.

A funeral wagon, painted in gold and red, with a dragon's eye to see the way to heaven for its occupants, carried the five urns. The inside of the wagon was festooned with purple and white ribbons and purple pillows, each pillow holding a photograph of one of the monks. The photographs would be displayed in the pagoda of the monks, honoring their memory. All Vietnamese keep a very formal photograph of themselves hidden away, so that their family may display it on the mantel in their home after their death. The photographs are never displayed until then.

Professional wailers, funeral bands, and hundreds of saffron-robed monks formed a shuffling procession behind the funeral wagon. The citizens of the city stood along the side of the street watching quietly. Theirs was not the usual detached curiosity. There was instead a very strong sense of involvement with the funeral procession. It was as if everyone, from the oppressed scholar, to the harassed petty crook, was aware that the monks had somehow given their lives for them.

Ordinarily such a procession would be in violation of the law. The activities of the Buddhists were tightly controlled. However, in a move toward appeasement, President Diem had temporarily suspended many of the sanctions, and the religious leaders of Saigon had quickly organized the funeral procession.

The National Police, the Special Police, and many uniformed members of the army stood by, watching the parade. None made an effort to interfere, and in fact many of them made gestures of respect as the funeral passed by. In Saigon, for the moment, time stood still.

## 3

THE VILLAGE OF HOA GINH WAS PROUD OF THE XA HOA Pagoda. The pagoda was not only their church, it was their social center as well. It was the largest and most beautiful Buddhist temple in the entire province.

In the Xa Hoa Pagoda, in Hoa Ginh, that very night the village faithful had gathered to burn their joss sticks and to make their offerings to Buddha. The air hung heavy with the sweet smell of incense, and the sound of prayer chants echoed melodiously through the cavernous red and gold temple.

No one paid any attention to the convoy of vehicles when they rolled through the street of the village, because the army frequently conducted maneuvers in the area. The lead Jeep had a two-way radio, and messages coming over it were so loud that they rolled across the landscaped garden of the pagoda like voices from a loudspeaker. But even that didn't cause undue disturbance among the villagers.

The convoy stopped, and white-helmeted soldiers poured out of the trucks. Officers shouted commands and gave orders, and the men formed into precise military platoons. This was unusual, so the people stopped and began to watch them.

Colonel Doung had been in the lead Jeep, and he walked along the line of vehicles until he stood in the middle, where he remained to watch the junior officers getting the soldiers into formation. A little girl stepped up to him and jerked his pants leg. When Doung looked down she held her hand out, palm up, already an expert in the art of begging. Doung ignored her.

"Colonel, the detail is formed," one of the officers reported. Doung returned the officer's salute, then raised his arm to look at his watch. For several moments there was an eerie tableau- vivant, illuminated by the brightness of the moon. Colonel Doung stood silently, his arm crooked, staring at his watch. The soldiers were in neat lines, absolutely motionless, faces devoid of all expression. The villagers appeared mesmerized by the scene, neither moving nor talking. The prayer chants and cymbals had stilled, and the village was in absolute quiet. The only sound was the flat clanking of a cowbell. It was hanging from the neck of a water buffalo that was tethered and grazing nearby. Occasionally a rush of static would pop over the two-way radio in the command Jeep. "Commence the operation," Doung said quietly. What happened next was totally unexpected, and everyone was rooted in shock, unable to react until it was too late. One of the officers shouted a command, and the neat military ranks surged forward, yelling and brandishing truncheons, attacking everyone.

The screams of fear and pain were drowned out by the sound of destruction as the buildings were set ablaze and the meager furnishings smashed.

In house after house, the hiding places of the most

prized possessions were discovered, and the treasures—perhaps a flashlight, a packet of steel needles, or an oil lantern—destroyed or stolen by the soldiers. The women begged and cried, and the men shouted in anger. But they were clubbed into insensibility.

Gradually the villagers were herded toward the pagoda, and soon practically all of them gathered inside, shaking in terror and rage.

A temporary truce seemed to have been called, because for several seconds there was no further activity on the part of the soldiers. Everything was silent save the continuous clanking of the cowbell as the buffalo quietly grazed, oblivious of the destruction going on around him.

Colonel Doung took a battery-powered loudspeaker and spoke to the people inside the pagoda.

"Attention! Attention! President Diem and the government of the Republic of Vietnam have declared that a state of martial law is in existence! One of the restrictions that has been placed on the people is the Pagoda Assembly Act. All buildings that are part and parcel of the Buddhist religion are to be used for religious purposes only. The gathering in such a building of anyone for political purposes is strictly prohibited. I now declare all who are gathered in the Xa Hoa Pagoda are there for political purposes and order that it be evacuated immediately."

Doung put the loudspeaker down, and a handful of terrorized citizens started to leave the pagoda. A squad of soldiers rushed at them and began beating them, forcing them back inside. Doung watched the proceedings impassively.

"You have only thirty seconds remaining in which to evacuate," Doung said over the loudspeaker again.

"I plead with you to do so at once!"

A few others tried to leave, but they, too, were driven back inside by the soldiers.

"You were warned, and your time has expired," Doung said.

Inside the pagoda the people were wild with terror. They knew now that the people outside wouldn't let them leave. They knew that they were all about to die.

"Look!" one of them cried out. He pointed to a hissing object that had been tossed in by one of the soldiers. That object was soon joined by several others, and then, with a popping sound, tear gas began spewing thickly, nauseatingly, from the small gray canisters.

The terror turned to hysteria, and the wheezing, crying mob surged for the doors. Many were cut down by rifle fire, others by skull-smashing blows, as the troops quieted them with grim efficacy. Fires licked at the night sky, and silhouetted against the orange flames, soldiers could be seen dumping buckets of feces from the community toilets into the community wells.

"Recall the detail," Colonel Doung ordered. Shouted commands from the officers brought the troops back to the trucks, where they climbed on board as calmly as boarding a bus. Doung pulled out a silk handkerchief and looked over the destroyed village as he wiped his hands. He climbed back into the lead Jeep and signaled for the convoy to leave.

When the convoy pulled out, they would leave behind a village in which practically every hut was burning. The screaming, shouting, and rattle of musketry had stilled. Now there was only the crying of a child, the snapping of the flames, and, as there had been throughout the whole nightmare, the flat clanking of the cowbell.

The stunned survivors stared at their destroyed village in disbelief as the trucks roared away.

Colonel Doung led the convoy down Highway 13 to their next stop, Di An. Di An was much larger than Hoa Ginh, so he wouldn't be able to sack and pillage the whole town. However, he had orders to destroy the pagoda and to bring back the patriarch of the Buddhist sect there, a priest named Vu Dinh Due.

The pagoda was on a square in the middle of the town, and as it burned, it created a glowing circle of light in the black of the night. Just beyond the wavering flames the people of the town gathered in a large crowd and stood in the protective cloak of darkness. They watched in fearful silence as the soldiers methodically destroyed the relics of the pagoda, some of which were more than a thousand years old. Colonel Doung kept glancing cautiously toward the crowd, alert for any possible uprising, but no one showed any sign of resisting.

"Colonel Doung, we cannot find Vu Dinh Due," one of the officers reported.

"Question some of the villagers," Doung ordered.

"We have captured three who were attempting to hide a relic. I questioned them, but they would say nothing."

"Bring them to me."

Colonel Doung had been leaning against his Jeep watching both the work of his men and the actions of the crowd that had gathered in the darkness. He walked to the center of the square and stood there, his feet spread apart, his hands on his hips. He looked at the fire and watched a piece of fire-blackened paper tumble crazily as it rode a column of heat and smoke high into the night sky.

"Here are the three men," the young lieutenant said, pushing three sullen men along in front of him.

Doung looked at them for a moment. Their hands had been tied behind their backs. There were marks on their faces from where they had been beaten.

"Do you know where Vu Dinh Due is?" Doung asked calmly.

"Yes, but we'll not turn him over to dogs," the one in the middle said.

Doung looked at the one who had spoken. He was taller than Doung. His features and the look of pride and determination on his face were a classic representation of the Vietnamese idea of what a folk hero should look like.

"You will not tell us?" Doung asked, and his question was delivered in an almost apologetic tone of voice.

"No," the young man spat. "Never." Doung pulled his pistol from his holster and pointed it at the man. He pulled the trigger without saying another word, and the pop of the .45 echoed through the square. The young man was pitched back, dying with a look of surprise on his face.

"Will you tell us?" Doung asked the second of the two prisoners. His voice was agonizingly calm.

The second man looked at his dead comrade, and then at Doung. His body began to jerk convulsively and his lips trembled.

Doung shot him, and then turned his gun on the last of the three.

"I will tell, I will tell!" the third one began yelling. He cried, and begged that his life be spared, and sank to his knees in supplication.

Doung put his pistol back in the holster and looked at

the lieutenant. "I don't believe you'll have any trouble now," he said with an evil grin.

"Thank you, Colonel," the lieutenant said, grabbing his prisoner roughly.

Colonel Doung wiped his hands with his silk handkerchief again and returned to his Jeep, where he pulled out a clipboard and studied the operational orders Nhu had given him. Doung's raids tonight were only a small part of an operation that was taking place across the entire country. Nhu had assured Doung that this would settle the Buddhist question once and for all.

A few moments later a group of Doung's men returned, laughing and yelling obscenities at an old man they were leading. They had a rope tied around his neck. The man was around eighty-five, hollow-cheeked and extraordinarily frail. His skin had the texture of parchment, and the hair of his beard was as fine as threads of silk. His eyes were downcast, but he did not wear the look of fear as he stood before Doung. This was man they were looking for.

"Throw him in the truck," Doung ordered. "We must take him prisoner."

Vu Dinh Due was dragged to the last truck in the convoy and thrown on board. Then, his night's work finished, Doung ordered the convoy back to Saigon.

BACK IN SAIGON, Le stretched on perfumed sheets in the quiet of her own bedroom, unaware of the activities of her husband. The silver light of the moon splashed in through the window, projecting shadows on the walls in intricate patterns of lace.

Le occupied her mind by composing haiku, poems of exactly seventeen syllables. When they are perfectly constructed they are like pebbles cast into the pool of the mind, sending out ripples of association.

A fallen flower…returning to the branch? …It was a butterfly.

Then, while she was totally immersed in her thoughts and almost oblivious of her surroundings, Doung banged the door open and turned on the lights.

The room was flooded in the harsh white glare, and the world of escape Le had created for herself vanished immediately.

"Doung, what is it? What is wrong?" Le asked, sitting up quickly and pulling the sheet to her chin. She didn't normally share a room with her husband, and his entry at any time was a rare occurrence. At this hour it was unheard of.

Doung looked at Le, and the expression on his face frightened her. He held his hands out to her. "I have blood on these hands," he said excitedly.

Le looked at his hands in confusion. They were clean. "What are you talking about? There is no blood."

"Smell them," Doung ordered. He sat on the edge of the bed and thrust his hands beneath Le's nose.

Le noticed nothing about his hands, but his clothes smelled of smoke.

"What a grand day!" Doung said, his eyes looking just over Le's head as if he were seeing something in the distance.

Le pulled the sheet about her more tightly and moved across the bed. She had never seen Doung like this. It was terrifying. "Doung, what are you talking about?"

Doung looked at Le, and for an instant the almost insane glow left his eyes. He answered her calmly.

"Nhu ordered a nationwide crackdown on the Buddhists tonight. The Can Lao arrested or killed more than fourteen-hundred of them. It will break the back of their resistance once and for all."

"And you did this thing too?" Le asked. "You are Buddhist."

"I am Vietnamese," Doung said vehemently. "And tonight I proved it. I destroyed one entire village, and the pagoda in Di An."

"You destroyed a village?" Le asked, terror beginning to creep into her voice.

"A small village of no consequence. It is known as Hoa Ginh.

"Hoa Ginh?" Le gasped. "But no!"

"Why are you so concerned about a mere village?"

"The people of Hoa Ginh helped me today. And you destroyed their village? All those people are now homeless?"

Doung laughed, but it was more like a short explosive sneer. "Don't worry, there aren't too many people homeless, because there aren't too many people left. Most were killed."

Le buried her face in her hands, and began to sob, her tears a mixture of sorrow, terror, and revulsion.

Le took a bath, making the water much hotter than she normally would, trying to scald away the unclean feeling. When she was finished, she went upstairs to one of the guest rooms. She locked herself inside, then collapsed across the bed and cried until just before dawn, when she fell asleep from exhaustion.

## 4

IN HIS APARTMENT OVER ON CONG LY, JUSTIN WAS waking up at about the same time Le was falling asleep. It was still dark outside. It was too early even for the dawn people. Justin would not normally have been awake yet, but the section of Saigon in which he lived was experiencing one of the frequent electrical failures, and the fans had stopped.

The heat began collecting in Justin's bedroom, enveloping him in its oppressive weight and bathing him in perspiration. With no breeze to keep them blown away, the mosquitoes began. They are so tiny that they can land, make several bites, and then fly away before the victim ever realizes it. Their bites can't be felt, but the anticoagulant toxin they inject to allow the blood to be sucked up is powerful, and the irritation and itching of ten to twenty bites erupting at nearly the same time is maddening.

Justin awoke with his nerves raw from the itching. He sought some relief by taking a shower. Then he took a bath in mosquito repellent, using two whole bottles.

The repellent had an unpleasant odor and caused his skin to feel a slight burn, but it kept the mosquitoes off.

He tried to go back to bed, but there wasn't a breath of air moving in his room, and the contact of the sheet with his repellent-soaked skin seemed to make the burning sensation more noticeable. After a few minutes he walked out onto the porch—actually a balcony, since his apartment was on the third floor.

There was a slight breeze, so Justin opened a Coke and sat on his balcony naked, taking advantage of what little air there was.

By the time he had finished his Coke the city began waking up, and the morning people had begun their rounds. Justin watched the birth of the new day. Before the sun rises in Vietnam the eastern sky is spread with a great palette of color, starting with purple and dark blue, then turning to red, orange, yellow, and finally the silver of day as the sun disc becomes completely visible.

Justin looked down on the street and watched an old woman set up her portable sidewalk cafe on the corner of Cong Ly and Duong Truong Tan Buu. Cong Ly, Duong Truong Tan Buu, Tru Minh Ky, Thru Minh Gaing, Le Loi —all are streets in Saigon, and all were as intimately known to Justin as the streets of his home-town. In fact, Justin chuckled to himself, Saigon was his home town. Much more so than Jackson, Mississippi. The streets of Jackson—Bailey Avenue, Fortification, Poindexter, Capitol—were only names to him now. Try as he might, he could no longer match vivid images with the individual streets. The only image Justin could still recall was the image of the Baptist orphanage, where he had been raised. His parents had been killed when he was very young, leaving him and his sister orphans. If

Justin had any family other than his sister, he was unaware of it.

Actually, he had seen his sister only twice in the last thirty years. She had been adopted soon after they were orphaned. Her new parents didn't think it good for Ellen to have any ties with her past, and they moved away so that Justin could not see his sister. He saw her once, when she was eleven, and again, many years later, when Ellen had married and had children of her own. The last meeting had been awkward, and although Justin actually had two weeks' leave time, he had lied and told Ellen and her husband that he had only a few hours. They exchanged Christmas cards now, but she was little more to him than the St. Louis postmark on the envelope.

Justin left his balcony and his musing reluctantly and got dressed for work. Normally his office was in the Special Police headquarters building. Today, however, he would be going to the American Embassy as one of the contingent of officers greeting Henry Cabot Lodge, the newly appointed ambassador to Vietnam.

Brigadier General Andrew W. McKenzie was standing in front of the embassy, waiting with the others for the ambassador's car to arrive from the airport.

"Did you go by your office this morning?" McKenzie asked when Justin arrived.

"No, Sir," Justin answered. "Why?"

"The shit has really hit the fan. Last night the Vietnamese Army raided pagodas from Da Nang to the Delta."

"What?" Justin gasped in disbelief. "The army did it?"

"That's what our reports say."

"I can't believe it was the army. Maybe the Can Lao, or one of the branches.

Maybe even the National Police, but the army has openly supported the Buddhists."

"They are going to take the ambassador on a tour through the city this morning. I don't imagine he will be too pleased," McKenzie said.

"How did you find out about it?" Justin asked.

"General Le Quang Tung called the duty officer last night and reported it to him. We drove down to the Xa Hoa Pagoda and checked it out. They made a shambles of it down there. You can still see bloodstains."

"But Tung is one of Nhu's men. Why would he report it?" Justin questioned.

"I don't know," McKenzie answered. "Maybe he's getting sick of it himself. Damn, why the hell did it have to be the army?"

"Here comes the ambassador!" someone called, and the group that had assembled to greet him prepared for his arrival.

The ambassador's car was preceded and followed by Jeeps with flashing red lights. A policeman stood in the front seat of the lead Jeep blowing a whistle and waving traffic to the side with vigorous arm movements.

The car stopped in front of the embassy building, and Justin could see several curious Vietnamese watching from a distance, as well as the American military, and members of the embassy staff. Lodge walked from his car to the building, smiling a greeting at his reception, but obviously troubled by what had happened. Justin was standing nearby, and he heard one of the briefing staff members inform the ambassador that their phones were temporarily out of order but would be working again shortly.

There was a reception of sorts set up for the ambassador—coffee and small cakes, but Justin managed to avoid it, because he hated such social gatherings. He ducked out through one of the back entrances and went to his office, where he hoped to question Colonel Doung about the events of the night before. But when he arrived, he found that Doung wasn't there.

Since Justin had missed the reception coffee, he brewed a pot for himself, and had just poured a cup when the telephone rang.

"Justin, this is Le. I must see you at once," Le said, her voice tinged with a note of desperation.

"Of course," Justin replied. "What's wrong?"

"Something terrible has happened. Doung has destroyed Hoa Ginh, the village that helped us yesterday."

"Then it wasn't the army," Justin exclaimed to himself.

"Justin, please! I must go there and help if I can. Will you take me?"

"Yes, of course," Justin answered at once. "I would like to go there too. I'll come by and pick you up."

"No!" Le answered sharply. "I want to leave this house before my husband awakens. I'll meet you at the Hotel Caravelle."

"I'll be waiting there for you," Justin promised.

Justin hung up the phone and thought about what Le had just told him. He had been certain this morning that the army wasn't involved, but he had had nothing to go on but his own certainty. Now, however, he would be able to get proof, and then he could return to General McKenzie with the truth.

Justin parked his Jeep on the curb directly in front of the hotel. The Caravelle is the most beautiful and the most elegant hotel in Vietnam. Its guests are almost exclusively members of the press, and Justin could not help but chuckle to himself when he read the dispatches of some of the correspondents.

They frequently bore a dateline such as "In the field with the Fifth Special Forces," and they would describe the jungle heat, the mosquito's sting, and the bomb's terror, all from the fertile imagination of the writers, many of whom strayed no farther from their rooms than the hotel's eighth-floor bar.

Justin bought a couple of Vietnamese-language newspapers and looked through them for news of the raids, but he found nothing. He had just finished when Le slipped into the seat beside him without a word. He almost didn't recognize her. She was wearing dark glasses and the black pajama-type garb worn by both sexes of the peasant class.

When they reached the village, they saw that every house in Hoa Ginh had been damaged. The mud walls of the simple huts wouldn't burn, but they were blackened from the fire that had consumed the straw roofs and wooden frames and furniture. The few Vietnamese who had survived stood in pathetic groups around a small charred area in the center of the square. The charred area was the remains of the rice supply for the entire village. Doung's men had been very thorough. They had soaked it with gasoline before they burned it.

The village was without food or water, but it was also nearly out of people. No more than ten or twelve had remained through the night. Now they wandered around in a daze, sifting through the rubble, trying to fit the pieces of their lives together again.

Many of the dead had been carried away by their families, but there were still forty-three bodies drawn together, lying in neat rows in the middle of what had been the marketplace.

Justin looked at the bodies. Most had been shot, but a few had crushing skull wounds, as if they had been killed by severe head blows.

One of those killed was the same old woman who had dressed Le's wounds. She was clutching three corners of a cloth parcel. The fourth corner had dropped down, exposing the contents of the parcel. There was a faded photograph in an imitation gold frame, two spools of thread, and a small packet of letters. Justin looked for the scissors that had been such an obvious source of pride for the old woman, but they weren't there.

"Why did the army do this?" one of the survivors asked Justin. "I told the army, 'We are loyal, here,' but they shoot and burn and kill and listen to no one."

"Why do you say it was the army?" Justin asked.

"They wore the leopard uniforms of the army," the man said resolutely.

"It was not the army," Le said in English so the man wouldn't understand her. "It was Doung and the Special Police."

"Le, why are you so sure?"

"Because this morning he spoke of it. He bragged of the killings and the beatings—" Le paused in her commentary, and a slight shiver passed over her.

As she spoke, she sobbed quietly and tears slid down her cheeks. Justin felt a tremendous rage developing inside him at the cruelty towar these innocent villagers who had been so helpful to him and Le the day before.

Justin and Le worked with the villagers, digging from the rubble whatever could be salvaged. Later in the day friends and relatives from nearby villages brought food, and they ate a communal dinner, sitting on the ground around a large straw mat. Justin sat cross-legged with the others and worked his chopsticks expertly as he conveyed to his mouth rice and little pieces of fish seasoned with the extremely pungent nuoc mam sauce.

"Why are you, an American, helping us?" one of the villagers asked Justin as they ate.

"I feel a great evil was done here, and I want to help," Justin answered. "The fact that I am an American has nothing to do with it."

"But the Americans are here to oppress our religion and customs," the villager said.

"Perhaps the Viet Cong say this, but that isn't so," Justin replied.

"But the Americans say this," the old man insisted. He put his rice bowl down and reached into his back pocket to pull out a folded piece of paper, which, Justin realized, must be a propaganda leaflet. At the top of the leaflet there was a crossed American flag and a South Viet- namese flag. There was also a drawing of an American GI shaking hands with a Vietnamese soldier. A line in English stated that the leaflet was a product of the "United States Army Psychological Warfare Unit." Every- thing else was in Vietnamese.

"Read this, please," the old man offered, handing the paper to Justin.

*Citizens of Vietnam. The United States is here to help your country. We will show no mercy to members of the Viet Cong or to their lackeys, the militant Buddhists, whose activities aid the Communist cause. We back the legitimate government in its just battle against Buddhist extremism.*

The text was written in Vietnamese, but there were words, such as "lackeys," which even in translation would not be normal American expressions. Justin suspected that the document was a fake.

"You have been deceived, old one," Justin said. "This paper was forged—to make it look as if the Americans printed it. But I saw the American ambassador this morning. His face was saddened because of the violence last night."

"There is an old Vietnamese saying," the man said. "'Look not to a man's face for his thoughts but to his heart.'"

"It is a wise saying," Justin agreed.

The old man put his hand on Justin's shoulder. "I can see your heart, my friend, and I know that it is good. But I fear that even you do not know the heart of your own people. Perhaps you are no longer one of them. Perhaps you are now one of us."

Justin thought about what the old man said. Perhaps he was right. Perhaps Justin was no longer one of the Americans. He certainly didn't share the same attitude as many of them. Perhaps Justin's entire psyche was now so attuned to ideographic symbolism, so aware of the shades of difference, that he was no longer able to filter out everything but black and white, as did the Americans.

Heat lightning flashed, rose-colored, inside the whipped-cream mountain of cloud banks rising from the northeast. A change in the wind brought with it the smell of rain, and the women began gathering things to get them to shelter. Justin reached out and took Le's hand.

"We must go," he said. "I must report to General McKenzie."

## 5

THE NEXT MORNING THE PHONES RANG CONSTANTLY IN the large villa at the junction of Tru Minh Ky and Railroad Number Six. That was the headquarters of General Andrew W. McKenzie, Chief of the Southeast Asia Operational Planning country team.

The phone calls were from the embassy, and MACV and they started as soon as word spread that McKenzie had been summoned to the White House for a special meeting because of the pagoda raids. Barclay was right. The Diem regime was behind them, and not the ARVN.

"Yes, I imagine I will see the President," McKenzie spoke into the phone. "I'll keep it in mind, but you must remember I'll be there only for a few hours, and then I'm coming right back."

McKenzie drummed his fingers on the desk impatiently, and wished that the caller would hang up. Finally, McKenzie cut him off by saying that he was too rushed to talk. McKenzie hung up the telephone and looked down at a list of things that had to be done before he left for Washington.

He had only five days allocated for the trip. It would take a day to get there and another day to come back, so his time in Washington would be very limited. And now that knowledge of his trip had leaked out, it seemed as if every American in Saigon had a personal message for McKenzie to take with him. The phone rang again.

"David, get in here and start answering some of these damn phone calls!" McKenzie shouted to his aide, who was busy in the next room.

Lieutenant David Kaplan came in quickly, picked up the phone, and talked quietly into it.

McKenzie looked at Kaplan, and an involuntary shudder of disgust passed over him. Kaplan was not only McKenzie's aide, he was also his son-in-law. McKenzie's daughter, Barbara, had married Kaplan in college, raving about what a brain he was. He had achieved many scholastic honors, and was truly an intellectual.

Perhaps he is an intellectual, but he doesn't have any common sense at all, McKenzie thought. And besides, he was a Jew.

David hung up the phone and looked over at the General. He cleared his throat hesitantly before he spoke, like a swimmer testing water.

"Yes, David, what is it?" McKenzie asked, sighing.

"It was from MACV. They want you to stop by and see them before you leave."

"Ha," McKenzie said. "There's a fat chance of that. I'm busier now than a cat covering shit on a freeway. There isn't time in my schedule for one more thing."

McKenzie looked at his watch. "Have you made arrangements for the plane?"

"Yes, sir," David said. "General, are you sure I can't go with you? Barbara could meet us in Washington."

43

"We won't have time for that," McKenzie said. "I'm not even going to call them."

"It isn't right that you should get that close and not contact your family."

"David," McKenzie said in exasperation, "you are an intelligent young man. You can see what is going on over here. We've got a crisis on our hands! The Diem raids on the Buddhists have changed the entire picture, and I'm going back tonight to report on it. It's a critical assignment, and nothing must interfere with it. You do understand, don't you?"

"Yes sir," David said.

"Good. You keep your eyes and ears open for me while I'm gone, and report to me when I get back." McKenzie looked at his watch again. "Where the hell is that idiot driver of mine?" he asked irritably.

"Sir, you've got plenty of time," David said, surprised at the General's agitation. "Your plane doesn't leave for quite a while."

"I've got something else to do," McKenzie said. The phone rang again. "Damn," McKenzie swore. "You tell everyone, even if it's Lodge or Harkins, that I've already left."

David grabbed the phone as McKenzie walked impatiently outside to wait for his car.

There was one thing remaining on his schedule. One thing that others might not understand, but something that was very important to McKenzie. Something that he had to do to relieve the terrible tension building up inside him. Tension that could only be relieved in the villa of Antoine Mouchette.

Antoine Mouchette was a Frenchman who had been born in Vietnam, as had his father before him. Despite the geography of his birth, Antoine wrapped himself in his French heritage and culture as securely as the most patriotic citizen of France.

Antoine was the third generation to own and operate the Frankindochin Rubber Company, a complex of rubber plantations and processing plants that supplied a major portion of the world's raw rubber. It was an extremely profitable operation, and Antoine was one of the few in whose hands most of the wealth of Vietnam rested.

A select group of these moneyed Frenchmen, the inner-corps, had formed a close-knit organization known as the France-Cochin-Societe. The expressed purpose of the FCS was to promote the welfare and social well-being of French nationals residing in Vietnam. The actual purpose was to provide expensive, and exotic diversions for the Societe members. Gambling, intrigue, and financial manipulations on an international scale were carried on by the Societe. But perhaps the most sought-after and the most available commodities were the pleasures of the flesh. It was in pursuit of the latter that McKenzie intended to make a call on Antoine before he left for his whirlwind trip to report to Washington.

Antoine had been called the master pimp of the Orient, but instead of taking offense, he had accepted this as his due. He felt it his duty to the Societe to outdo himself in the procurement of girls. Just being pretty wasn't enough. They had to be beautiful, cultured, and possess some other trait of unique desirability. Antoine attempted to make the unattainable attainable, but only for select members. Therefore, it was not unusual to see an internationally famous actress or a daughter of one of the wealthiest and most influential families in the world turn up as one of Antoine's "special" guests.

Of all Antoine's girls Tamara was the most special. She could rightfully claim the title of princess, because her father was king of a tiny European principality. The economic condition of the tiny country was entirely dependent on tourism and the continued good graces of the government of France, but the royal bloodline was authentic and stretched unbroken for several hundred years. Tamara had been next in line for succession to the throne, as no male heirs had been born. Then, when Tamara was sixteen, her mother died and her father remarried, this time a wealthy, beautiful, American film star. The new marriage produced the prince her father had always wanted, and Tamara was moved to the background, no longer the successor to the crown.

Tamara was sent to the United States for schooling, where she married and subsequently divorced an American, in defiance of her father's specific wishes. An abortion and her involvement with a married man, which wound up in court and on the pages of newspapers around the world, created the greatest scandal ever to occur in her father's small kingdom. Tamara's conduct caused her father to take the extreme and very rare action of *ex-purger de Vavbre genealogique*—expulsion from the family tree.

Tamara found herself disowned and penniless. She was an anachronism, a princess in a world grown too old for fairy tales. But she had four assets. She was beautiful. She was also of royal blood, albeit disenfranchised, and she had her wits and courage. But her most valuable asset was that she knew Antoine Mouchette, whose reputation had reached her long before she had left for America. Tamara knew that Antoine would be able to employ her, so she went to Saigon to look him up.

Antoine could scarcely believe his fantastic luck

when he realized that Tamara was just who she claimed to be. He kept her out of circulation for quite a while, not wanting to use his most special girl until he could realize a maximum advantage from her. Finally, the opportunity to use her presented itself in the person of General Andrew W. McKenzie.

McKenzie had visited Mouchette's villa on several occasions and Antoine had provided him with girls, but he had done nothing more than study McKenzie for the first few visits. He needed to know if McKenzie's personality was such that it could be exploited, and he needed to decide if McKenzie was in a position to be of benefit to him. In both cases the answer was yes, and so on the visit today McKenzie would meet Princess Tamara for the first time.

McKenzie rode in the back of his air-conditioned staff car, shielded from the hot afternoon sun by the darkly tinted glass, and enveloped by the deeply cushioned seat. Neither the smell, the noise, nor the heat could penetrate the big car as it glided majestically along the streets of the city. It moved confidently through the sputtering cyclos, the darting taxis, and the numerous military vehicles with as much authority as Moses parting the seas.

General McKenzie's villa was comfortable, but compared with the estate of Antoine Mouchette, McKenzie's villa was a pauper's shack. Passing through the walls that protected Mouchette's grounds from the outside was like Alice passing through the looking glass. Exquisitely tended gardens, cool splashing fountains, and well-fed beautiful people created a new world. McKenzie was affected the same way every time he came. He could feel his blood pressure increasing, and anticipation of what lay in store for him knotted his stomach.

The car came to a stop beneath a portico. "Meet me back here in two hours," McKenzie told his driver.

The car door was opened by a bikini-clad blonde whose voluptuousness threatened to spring free of the brief attire.

"Monsieur Mouchette welcomes you, mon General," the girl said seductively.

"Where is he?" McKenzie asked.

"In the library," the girl answered, her French accent making even that simple statement a pleasure to the ears. Mouchette greeted McKenzie with a drink and a smile, and beckoned for McKenzie to have a seat.

Mouchette was wearing a white silk suit and a lime-green shirt. Despite the fact that he was internationally known as a connoisseur of fine food and his every meal was a gourmet's delight, he had maintained a trim figure and was able to add his good looks to the other long list of qualifications that made him a successful playboy.

"I am glad you could make it tonight, General McKenzie," Antoine said smoothly. "There is someone I would like you to meet, a delightful young creature who also happens to be a genuine princess."

McKenzie laughed. "What am I supposed to do, put a glass slipper on her foot? I don't need a princess. You know what I want."

"Don't judge too quickly," Antoine said, "—at least not until you've seen her."

As Antoine finished talking, Tamara came into the room. She smiled at Antoine, and then greeted McKenzie with her hand outstretched, palm down, regally.

McKenzie was quite unprepared for her beauty. She

had long, soft blonde hair, which fell loosely across her shoulders, framing her face, giving it a look of deceptive purity. Emerald eyes set beneath delicately arched eyebrows and lips that were full and sensual tended to contradict the theme of innocence—and the girl was smiling as if she could read McKenzie's very thoughts.

"I— I— How do you do?" McKenzie stammered.

"I don't know, General. How will I do?" Tamara asked. Her English was perfect, but there was just the suggestion of a French accent, a subtle softening of the words, which tended to caress the language. And still there was that smile, a beautiful twinkling of the eye that made it appear as if she were drawing intense pleasure from the situation.

McKenzie looked at Antoine and tried to speak, but he couldn't. Finally, he made a gesture toward Tamara with his hand, asking the question with his eyes.

"Yes, General," Antoine replied, laughing patronizingly. "She's all yours."

McKenzie tried to speak, but his mouth was dry and his tongue was thick, and he couldn't make the words. Tamara laughed again and took his hand in hers, leading him from the library into a nearby bedroom.

"This is what you wanted, isn't it?" she asked, her huge emerald eyes pools of false innocence.

"Are you really a princess?" McKenzie asked.

Tamara laughed and brushed her blond hair away from her eyes with a long, graceful hand. "What do you think?"

"I think you are a queen," McKenzie said.

"I'll be anything you want," Tamara said, putting her arms around McKenzie's neck and pulling him to her for a kiss.

## 6

SAIGON WAS TEEMING WITH TENSION DURING THE TIME
General McKenzie was in Washington. Many of the
Vietnamese generals who had been quietly critical of the
Diem government had now become openly so, and talk
of trouble between the Vietnamese military and the
Diem government was common.

There was a reception at the American Embassy
three days after General McKenzie had left for Washington, and the buzzing conversation among the partygoers
dealt with the critical situation in Saigon. David Kaplan
attended it, so that he could tell McKenzie what the tone
of the conversation was.

Invariably when the conversation got around to the
military and to the generals who were against Diem,
the guests began talking about General Le Van Tung.
Tung had been one of Diem's most trusted generals,
and then quite suddenly he had suffered a loss of pres-
tige and power. Tung's fall from grace had superseded
even the pagoda raids as the prime topic of discussion,
and in the small American community, where gossip

was a leading source of entertainment, rumors ran rampant.

General Tung was at the party, and he stood quietly and alone on one side of the banquet hall smoking cigarettes and nursing a drink. David watched him from across the room for nearly an hour, and not one person had approached Tung to speak with him.

"Have you heard anything from your boss?" a voice suddenly asked.

David turned quickly, and saw a lieutenant, one of Stillwell's aides, standing at the bar waiting for a drink. "Did Stillwell send you over here to pump me for information?" David asked.

"You know better than that," Stillwell's aide said. He laughed. "But old Joe is about to bust a gut trying to figure out what's going on. Why was McKenzie called? Is he going to report directly to Kennedy?"

"I don't know," David answered. "I really don't. It came up so fast, there was very little time for discussion."

"Maybe Kennedy is about to give him the ax, like Diem did that little man over there," Stillwell's aide said. He pointed at Tung with the same hand that held his drink. "If that's so, you'd better start looking for a new job," the aide said with a laugh as he walked away.

David watched the tall lieutenant melt into the crowd, then looked back over to Tung, but Tung was gone. Or seemed to be. He surprised David by suddenly appearing right beside him.

"Your General's trip has caused some excitement and interest," Tung said.

"Uh—yes, sir, I suppose it has," David answered. "Do you have any idea of the purpose of his visit?' Tung asked.

"No, sir, not really."

Tung smiled. "But of course, you wouldn't be able to tell me even if you did know. Especially not now, since I've been given my new job as military advisor." Tung screwed up his mouth sarcastically as he said the words. "You'll have to excuse a foolish man for making conversation," Tung concluded.

"General, what happened?" David asked. Then, as if surprised at his own audacity in asking such a question, he covered his mouth with his hand. "Forgive me, it was very rude of me to ask."

Tung laughed. "Not at all, I've always admired the American trait of candor. I disagreed rather vehemently with Diem's Buddhist policy. It is not healthy to disagree with one's President in a situation such as we have here."

"I suppose not," David replied, not knowing what else to say.

An orderly approached then, and David was relieved to be called away.

Tung lit a cigarette, then drifted toward the door. He had accomplished what he had set out to do.

## 7

WHEN GENERAL MCKENZIE STEPPED OFF THE PLANE IN Saigon five days later, he was exhausted from his trip. He was hot and sweating and uncomfortable as he slid into the back seat of the staff car that had come to meet him. But, despite his exhaustion, he was elated.

He opened his briefcase and removed a folder. The folder contained the text of a cable that President Kennedy had sent to Ambassador Lodge, and McKenzie had been given a copy to carry with him before he left Washington. McKenzie read the cable again:

> It is now clear that whether the military proposed martial law or whether Nhu tricked them into it, Nhu took advantage of its imposition to smash pagodas with police and Doung's Special Police loyal to him, thus placing onus on military in eyes of world and Vietnamese people. Also, clear that Nhu has maneuvered himself into commanding position.
>
> U.S. Government cannot tolerate situation in which power lies in Nhu's hands. Diem must be given the chance to

rid himself of Nhu and his coterie and replace them with best military and political personalities available.

If, in spite of all your efforts, Diem remains obdurate and refuses, then we must face the possibility that Diem himself cannot be preserved.

We now believe immediate action must be taken to prevent Nhu from consolidating his position further. Therefore, unless you, in consultation with Harkins, perceive overriding objections, you are authorized to proceed along following line:

First, we must press on appropriate levels of Government of Vietnam (QVN) following line:

(a) USG cannot accept actions against Buddhists taken by Nhu and his collaborators under cover martial law.

(b) Prompt dramatic actions redress situation must be taken, including repeal of Decree 10, release of arrested monks, nuns, etc.

(2) We must at same time also tell key military leader that U.S. would find it impossible to continue support GVN militarily and economically unless above steps are taken immediately, which we recognize requires removal of Nhu from the scene. We wish to give Diem reasonable opportunity to remove Nhu, but if he remains obdurate, then we are prepared to accept the obvious implication that we can no longer support Diem. You may also tell appropriate military commanders we will give them direct support in any interim period of breakdown of central government mechanism.

(3) We recognize the necessity of removing taint on military for pagoda raids and placing blame squarely on Nhu.

*(4) You are authorized to have such statements made in Saigon as you consider desirable to achieve this objective. We are prepared to take same line here and to have Voice of America make statement along lines contained in next numbered telegram whenever you give the word, preferably as soon as possible.*

*Concurrently, with above, ambassador and country team should urgently examine all possible alternative leadership and make detailed plans as to how we might bring about Diem's replacement if should become necessary.*

*Assume you will consult with General Harkins re: any precautions necessary protect American personnel during crisis period.*

*You will understand that we cannot from Washington give you detailed instruction as to how this operation should proceed, but you will also know we will back you to the hilt on actions you take to achieve our objectives.*

*Needless to say; we have held knowledge of this telegram to minimum essential people and assume you will take similar precautions to prevent premature leaks.*

McKenzie closed the folder and smiled. He had accomplished just what he wanted.

Washington was now committed to a coup.

By now the car had come to a stop in front of his villa and his son-in-law met him at the driveway.

"How was the trip, General?"

"David, my boy, it couldn't have been better," McKenzie said, beaming, as he entered his villa.

"All of Saigon is talking about coup rumors," David said, following on McKenzie's heels. "And General Le Van Tung has been kicked out of power."

McKenzie slowed his quick strides and turned

around. "Well, what do you know! So, the first rat has left."

"What do you mean by that, sir?" David asked.

"Never mind."

"Would you like a drink, General?"

"No, no, not now," McKenzie said as he strode across the large room. "I've got to take care of this first. Get Colonel Rogers on the phone—tell him I want to meet with him tomorrow. Then call the embassy and MACV and set up appointments for me."

"Yes, sir," David answered.

McKenzie went into the cryptographic room and opened the safe reserved for classified documents. He logged the cable into the register, and then pulled out the encode book to select a name for the project. All operations have a code name so that they can be referred to or spoken about without compromising their subject. McKenzie found the day's date, then ran his finger down the list of code words until he came to the next available word. It was "Valkyrie."

"Valkyrie," McKenzie said, straightening up with a smile. "That has a good sound, a dramatic sound."

He had heard of Valkyrie somewhere. He pulled a dictionary off the shelf and looked up the word.

*Any of Odin's handmaidens who hover over battlefields choosing warriors to be victorious, and conducting the souls of the slain to Valhalla. "Chooser of the slain."*

McKenzie wrote the name on a tab index and affixed it to the folder. Then he made an entry in the book noting the fact that "Valkyrie" had been taken—and Operation Valkyrie was born.

## 8

THE TELEPHONE RANG SHRILLY IN MCKENZIE'S VILLA later that evening. He waited for his houseboy to answer it, then remembered that he had given him the night off.

Damn, McKenzie thought as he went over to answer it. His eyes widened in surprise when he heard the caller's name.

He listened for a while.

"Yes. Yes. I know all about it," McKenzie said.

He sat in a high wing chair in a room that was lighted only by the diffused glow of a lamp. He cupped the telephone between his chin and shoulder while he lit a cigarette. The flare of the match revealed his face intent on listening to his caller.

"No, I'm glad that you called."

There was a murmur of the voice from the other end.

"No. Don't worry. I'll be alone. Come to the back entrance and come disguised."

The call was concluded and McKenzie hung up the phone. He took a long drag on his cigarette and then put it out, his hand trembling from repressed excitement. A sputtering cycle turned off Tru Minh Ky and pulled to a stop behind McKenzie's villa. A small thin man stepped out of his seat, then pulled out a billfold to pay the driver his fare. When he took the billfold out, his hands shook, and he had to grip the wallet tightly to keep from dropping it. His fingers, which were stained yellow-brown by nicotine, even now held a cigarette. The little man counted out the money carefully, with no allowance for a tip. The cycle driver scratched his tightly muscled, varicose-veined leg stoically and accepted the money without comment, then drove off, his cycle laying down a screen of thick blue smoke.

The man started for the gate to McKenzie's quarters, where he was met by the General personally.

"Thank you for seeing me, General," the man said.

General McKenzie escorted his visitor into his office and offered him a seat in the dimly lit room. He held out a silver cigarette case and the man took a cigarette eagerly, lighting the new one from the butt of his old one.

"Tell me," General McKenzie said, leaning against the front of his desk, "what is on your mind?"

"I thought that perhaps we might have a mutual interest in the status of the Diem government," the man said.

"My interest is in what is best for Vietnam, as I am sure is yours," McKenzie said, sparring with his visitor.

"Ah—stability, yes," the visitor said. "But perhaps we agree that the Diem government is not best for Vietnam."

"And when did you come to this conclusion?" McKenzie asked. "After Diem stripped you of power? General Tung, you have long been one of Diem's most active supporters."

"That's where you are wrong," Tung said. "It is precisely because I have spoken against Diem, tried to countermand some of Nhu's anti-Buddhist policies, that I was relieved of my command. Now I'm forced to occupy a meaningless job."

"And so, in anger and revenge, you turn against him?" McKenzie asked.

Tung squinted up at McKenzie. "What difference do my reasons make? The fact is, I have a plan in mind. A plan that will require American support. And I think perhaps you received authority for such support on your recent trip."

"What is your plan?" McKenzie asked. Tung took a new cigarette from McKenzie's desk and lit it from the stub of his old one before he answered. He butted the old one in the highly polished brass shell casing that served as an ashtray. "I represent several concerned officers. At this moment, I don't wish to disclose all of their names; however, there are many of us. We believe that the time has come for a coup, and we are prepared to bring that about. But we want to know just where the United States stands?"

"You realize," McKenzie said cautiously, "that publicly we can't take a stand at all. We can't offer any encouragement."

"Public support without real help is like smoke without the fire," Tung said. "Will you help us?"

"I cannot pledge our support until I know your plans," McKenzie said. "I don't even know what you may want in the way of assistance."

"At this moment, I am content with your word to begin planning," Tung said. "Formulation of all our plans depends on the knowledge that we will have American support."

McKenzie smiled. "You may formulate your plans. As to United States support, we can discuss that more specifically when the time comes."

Tung stood and extended a bony hand. "You are a man of action and influence. I was right to come to you with this request, and I shall tell the others that we chose wisely."

McKenzie beamed under the praise from the South Vietnamese General and extended his hand almost benevolently. He had promised nothing, yet he had securely established himself as a key figure in the coup. After Tung left, McKenzie poured himself another drink and presented a silent toast to Operation Valkyrie.

After he left McKenzie's villa General Tung hurried back to his quarters, and then on to keep an important appointment.

General Tung elegantly attired in his dress uniform bore no resemblance to the man who had called on General McKenzie. Now he looked like the mandarin prince he was, and he waited in the reception hall of the presidential palace, where he was to meet Diem's brother, Nhu. As he waited, several uniformed girls, members of Madam Nhu's Young Women's Military Auxiliary, marched by. They saluted Tung, who remained seated, spurning what he considered foolishness.

"General Tung," Nhu greeted him a moment later. "Please come into my office. You saw my wife's girls? I believe she has developed a formidable force across the country," he said, laughing.

They went into the office, and Nhu shut the door, then came around and leaned against the front of the desk. "How did your meeting with General McKenzie go?" he asked.

Tung smiled. "You were right. You were right. Putting me in disfavor has made me very popular among the Americans. It was a stroke of genius on your part. I'll soon have them eating out of my hand."

Nhu folded his arms, then cupped his chin in his hand. His eyes narrowed as he looked at Tung. "So," he began, "what do you think? Will the Americans assist a coup?"

"Yes, I am sure of it," Tung said.

"Bastards!" Nhu swore, slamming his fist into his hand. "They come to our country, proclaim to the world that they are here to help us, and then behind our backs, they plot against us."

"Ask them to leave," Tung suggested.

"Only my brother can do that," Nhu said. "And he won't. He is too dependent on their aid, and too frightened of the consequences if they leave. Besides, I don't know if even he would be able to get them out now. I fear it is too late."

"Then what will you do, Excellency?" Tung asked.

Nhu smiled. "The same thing I've been doing since the Americans first arrived. Play them for the fools they are." Nhu laughed, and Tung joined him.

The Americans were almost childishly easy to trick. Their entire effort, political and military, depended on interpreters, and 99.9 percent of the interpreters were Vietnamese. The Vietnamese for the most part got their jobs with the Americans through the Saigon government. Therefore, the Vietnamese were all obligated to the Saigon government. That meant the words they spoke were the words the Saigon government wanted the Americans to hear.

A good example was the psychological-warfare leaflets. The United States was dropping millions of leaflets all over the country, and they had no idea at all of what was in the leaflets. They had prepared a text, which they supposed would be printed, but the final text had been approved by a Vietnamese. It was nothing like the original copy presented by the Americans.

"The Americans are like blind man's bluff," Nhu said. "They play with fire, but they are blind, mute, and deaf, and like the child in the game, stand still and swing wildly. We can easily avoid the swings."

"But the club they swing is a big one," General Tung warned.

Nhu laughed. "That is to our advantage also, since we will make sure that the club strikes our enemies. Once we get American support behind our phony coup, any other plotters will be put aside. The Americans would never support more than one coup plot."

"And after the plot is foiled? What then?" General Tung asked.

"Then the Americans will be exposed to the world for their betrayal. They will leave our country in disgrace, and then will try to buy our friendship with their aid programs."

General Tung grinned broadly, exposing his yellowed teeth and brown gums. "The Americans are their own worst enemy."

"They have an expression that fits this situation nicely," Nhu said. "They shall be hoist with their own petard."

Nhu laughed uproariously at the joke he was playing on the Americans, and General Tung joined him. They were still laughing when President Diem stepped in through the back door of Nhu's office, the door that led through a hallway to his own office.

"I am pleased that you can find something of amusement, my brother," Diem said rather curtly.

General Tung came to rigid attention at the sight of the President. He noticed that Diem was without shoes, and he tried not to look at his bare feet for fear of causing embarrassment.

"Why the long face, Diem?" Nhu asked, ignoring the remark Diem had made on his entrance.

"Have you listened to the Voice of America broadcasts? They are saying that your police raided the temples and pagodas."

"The Voice of America is not known as an organ of truth," Nhu said easily.

"Nor is the Can Lao," Diem replied. "But the point is, you neither silenced the Buddhists, as you said you would, nor did you place blame for the raids on the army. And now in the eyes of the world we stand accused of the vilest crimes. My foreign minister to Washington, your own father-in-law, has shaved his head and resigned his post in protest."

"He is a foolish, weak old man, and the Americans have frightened him into such a move," Nhu said.

Diem pulled at the bridge of his nose, as he always did in moments of stress. "I feel as if we are riding the whirlwind. We are headed for disaster."

"If you would listen to the Americans, all you need to do is get rid of me," Nhu said.

"I know," Diem said quietly.

"And?"

"I've no wish to do that."

"But you might?" Nhu asked.

Diem was quiet for several seconds before he spoke. "No. You are my brother, and I value your counsel. But, perhaps if your wife would make fewer public pronouncements—for example, her referring to these suicides as monk barbecues. She does us great harm."

Nhu laughed shortly. "I can understand the American's fear of woman, but you, my brother? Would you cower before her skirts?"

"That is not the question," Diem protested. "The question is the Americans. We must get along with the Americans or I feel they will be the instrument of our destruction."

Nhu smiled and looked at General Tung, who had been present for the entire scene but had remained silent. "I think, my brother," Nhu said with a knowing look at General Tung, "that we need not fear the Americans."

## 9

"TUNG?"

"General Le Van Tung, yes."

Colonel Rogers looked at McKenzie. "General, that's a brilliant stroke. How did you get him?"

"That's the best part of it," McKenzie said. "He came to see me last night. He needs us even more than we need him."

McKenzie got up and paced the room. Colonel Rogers watched him. As McKenzie's Chief of Staff, Rogers was frequently used as an advisor to the General. There were some, though, who considered him little more than a yes-man.

McKenzie stood looking out the window, then turned to look back at Rogers, who was sitting on a chair in front of the desk.

"Vern, do you know what it will mean to us if we are the successful architects of Valkyrie?"

"Yes, sir," Colonel Rogers replied. "And I'll certainly do my part."

"Good. I knew I could depend on you. I'm counting on you, of course, to head this project."

"General, I have an idea that might be helpful—if you don't mind a suggestion."

"A suggestion? Yes, by all means, let's hear it."

"We have ample evidence of the impact of our leaflet campaign," Colonel Rogers said. "Perhaps, through them we could prepare the population for the idea that a change in government is desirable. That would ensure popular support for Operation Valkyrie."

"An excellent suggestion," General McKenzie agreed. "The wording would have to be just perfect, though. We don't want to compromise Valkyrie before we are in a position to act."

"I'll write them myself," Colonel Rogers replied. "It's in my bailiwick, since I'm head of psy-war. I'll use my best interpreter for the translation."

"An American?" McKenzie asked, taking a cigarette from the silver box on his desk.

"No, sir, a Vietnamese," Colonel Rogers answered. "But one who speaks English perfectly. There will be no difficulty in making sure the shading comes through."

"How about Colonel Barclay?" General McKenzie suggested.

"I am satisfied with my own interpreter," Rogers replied stiffly.

"Vern, I know you don't like Barclay. And perhaps you would rather use your own interpreter. I won't interfere. But Barclay is going to be our middleman. I want him to be the go-between—reporting to you, of course. With Barclay in the middle, if something goes wrong with the operation, we could write him off as an individual acting without authority, and keep ourselves out of it."

66

"Colonel Barclay doesn't think too much of Tung," Rogers suggested. "Perhaps he would rather find someone else. Have you spoken with him?"

"Barclay will work with whomever we tell him to. There will be no individualism in this. It's a team operation, and Barclay will be a member of that team. I'll make that perfectly clear to him when I tell him." General McKenzie looked at his watch. "He should be here shortly. I sent Lieutenant Kaplan after him."

JUSTIN BARCLAY WASN'T at his apartment. He was at the My Kahn floating restaurant.

The My Kahn was a large white houseboat tied up at the Saigon docks, sharing berthing space with giant vessels of commerce and ships of war. A long, rickety gangplank stretches from the dock to the lower deck, and then stairs lead to the large open deck, which is the main dining room. The menus are divided into four sections, American, French, Vietnamese, and Chinese. The waiters are familiar with all four languages.

Justin had invited Colonel Doung and Le to eat with him, so he called Colonel Doung as soon as Doung had returned from Vung Tau, and issued the invitation.

Justin looked at his watch again and was about to conclude that Doung wouldn't come, when he heard the sirens.

The other diners in the restaurant moved to the rail nearest the street to see what the commotion was. Justin didn't move, because he knew what it was. Two motorcycle policemen, dressed all in white and with very wide leather belts, crash helmets, and large sunglasses masking their humanity, led the procession. They were followed by a Jeep, then a large black

Mercedes, then another Jeep, and two more motorcycle policemen.

In addition to the sirens, there were flashing red lights and blowing whistles.

An old woman had spread a bamboo mat out near the curb by the My Kahn. She had several wicker cages, and the cages contained live ducks and chickens. The approaching procession made no effort to avoid her, and at the last moment the old woman had to flee for her life. The vehicles struck the wicker cages, killing some of the fowl, freeing the others.

The ducks and chickens began beating their wings wildly, trying to get away. For the crowd, the old woman's misfortune had become their gain. Although they wouldn't have stolen the animals while they were penned, they now considered them free game, and the birds were all gathered up by the crowd in a matter of seconds.

Doung and Le had been in the Mercedes, and they stepped from the car and moved through the crowd of people toward the restaurant, oblivious of the invectives of the hysterical old woman.

"You made quite an arrival," Justin said when Doung and Le joined him at his table.

"I was detained a little longer than I anticipated," Doung said. "I thought an escort would help make up the time I lost."

"Doung, the old woman lost all her wares," Le said.

"The old woman is lucky," Doung said. "Suppose I had asked her for a tax receipt, to show that she has authority to sell on the streets. Do you suppose she would have had one?"

"She probably doesn't even know of the requirement," Le said.

"She could go to jail for six months. She is better off losing a few chickens."

"Let me tell you of my trip to Vung Tau," Doung said to Justin, smiling broadly and putting the incident of the old woman out of his mind entirely.

The waiter brought the soup as Doung was talking about his trip. Le was sitting on the same side of the table as Doung, next to the rail near the water. She was eating her soup with her head cast down. Occasionally she would look up, raising the great shutters of her eyelashes, to look at Justin. They had exchanged greetings only. Doung was monopolizing most of the conversation.

"Don't you agree?"

Justin suddenly heard Doung ask. "Agree?"

"My friend, you seem detached," Doung said, smiling. "You are still angry over the raids. And I thought this meal was to be a reconciliation."

"Yes, the raids made me angry," Justin said. "But aside from my personal feelings about the raids, I can't understand how Nhu could do such an unwise thing, since it created even greater ill will—and certainly made no friends in the American circles."

"But my men were dressed in army uniforms. That creates ill will for the army, and right now it is not to our benefit for the army to enjoy too much popular support —as you can readily understand."

"But the people were not fooled by the uniforms," Justin insisted. Even as Justin spoke, however, he remembered that the villagers of Hoa Ginh had been completely fooled.

"You are mistaken," Doung said. "You overestimate the intelligence of our peasants. Most of them still think it was our army."

"Doung, why did you do it?" Justin asked.

"The pagodas are natural hiding places for the Viet Cong," Doung said. "We have merely denied them that sanctuary."

Justin looked at Doung coldly. "Perhaps you are forgetting who you are talking to?"

Doung laughed, and put down the soup spoon, and took up his chopsticks. He gestured with them as he answered Justin.

"You are right. The Viet Cong threat is a formula answer. The real answer is that Nhu fears the Buddhists. He fears that they will mount a revolution that will sweep Diem from office."

"Do you think this?"

"Yes," Doung said. A mask of coldness descended over his face, and the twinkle of humor in his eyes disappeared. "We are not a popular government. My police are not a popular police force. But we are necessary. And, in order to function we must be ruthless and crush any movement of the Buddhists. They would make a revolution if they could."

A smile reappeared on Doung's face. Not a pleasant one, but one that was tinged with evil and irony. "All the wolves aren't in sheep's clothing," he said. "Some are dressed as the shepherds."

"Meaning the generals within your army?" Justin asked.

Doung's eyes narrowed until they were but two slits. "And yours," he suggested.

Le excused herself momentarily, and Justin knew that she was going to see the old woman and give her money. Doung made no effort to stop her, and after she had left, his humor returned and a genuine smile appeared. "Let's not talk of such things now," he suggested. "You should have come to Vung Tau with me. I inspected some of Madam Nhu's young virgin girl army while I was there." He said the words leeringly.

"That must have been interesting," Justin said.

"Interesting? Indeed, it was. As the inspecting officer, I was afforded certain—shall we say—privileges? I'll say this for Madam Nhu, she has done a great service for the inspecting officer. Where else could one find such a collection of young girls so anxious to do their duty? I chose a young girl of fifteen."

As Doung spoke, his eyes gleamed with a devil's lust. Justin felt himself shudder involuntarily. The thought of Doung with a fifteen-year-old girl was disgusting. "Wasn't she a little young?" Justin asked.

Doung laughed aloud and reached across the table to wag his finger slowly in Justin's face. "Colonel, you know our language, you know our customs, and you know our people. But sometimes you still show that you possess that peculiar Western morality that says young girls cannot be used. You deny yourself needlessly with such foolishness. Old women are for keeping house, young girls are for pleasure."

Le reached the table then, and took her seat without a word. She hadn't overheard any of the conversation, and Justin was glad for that. He began to think that perhaps this dinner wasn't such a good idea.

Justin looked out at the water, and at the large ark-shaped boats, which were actually sea-going vessels. They plied the coast of Vietnam carrying passengers, livestock, and cargo, all on a common deck inside the gymnasium-sized cabin.

A man was urinating off the side of one of the boats as it passed just a few feet away. He looked at the diners in the My Kahn with total unconcern over the fact that he was attending to one of his most personal acts. Just down the deck from the urinating passenger an old woman was dipping a bucket into the river to get water for cleaning the chicken she would be cooking for her family.

"Colonel Barclay?" an American voice said, and Justin looked around to see Lieutenant Kaplan.

"Yes, Kaplan, what is it?" Justin asked.

"Excuse me, sir," Kaplan said. "General McKenzie would like to see you at your earliest convenience."

"I'll call on the General as soon as I have finished dining," Justin said.

"Sir, excuse me, but he's having a meeting now, and would like you to attend."

"I'm not a member of his staff," Justin replied, a little irritated.

"I have a Jeep," Lieutenant Kaplan insisted.

"I have my own transportation," Justin snapped. "I'll be there when I have finished here. Do you understand, Lieutenant?"

"Yes, sir," Kaplan replied, swallowing in embarrassment. He saluted almost apologetically, and then turned to leave.

"Don't worry about us," Doung said with a small laugh. "McKenzie sounds quite anxious. Perhaps you'd better go see him."

"I might as well," Justin said gruffly. "Our evening seems ruined now. I wonder what he wants?"

Doung smiled a knowing smile. "I believe he is about to ask you to put on shepherd's clothing."

Justin suddenly began to put together some of the pieces of Doung's conversation. Doung knew something, and was playing with his knowledge the way a cat would with a mouse.

Justin started after Kaplan, but he had taken no more than two or three steps away from the table when the world seemed to explode. There was a deafening roar and a searing flash of light. Justin was hurled across the floor and slammed into one of the support columns, then buried beneath falling debris.

He pulled himself to an upright position and tried to look around the restaurant, but the smoke and dust hung heavily, obscuring his vision and burning his lungs with acridity.

His ears were still ringing from the sharpness of the explosion, so that he was only barely aware of the screams and cries of the injured and trapped.

Justin looked over to the table he had just left, and felt a sense of relief at seeing that Doung and Le were uninjured. Le was just sitting there, looking over the carnage in shock.

Lieutenant Kaplan had not been as lucky, and Justin drew his breath in sharply when he recognized the body near him. Kaplan lay in the middle of the wreckage of the spice table, his limbs and body twisted in a grotesque pattern and covered with the spices, as if he were being served up in some macabre dish.

## 10

JUSTIN LEANED AGAINST THE AMBULANCE THAT HAD BEEN supplied by the American army and drank a cup of coffee that had been supplied by the Vietnamese Red Cross. He had stayed to help with the rescue work after the terrorist bomb had destroyed the My Kahn restaurant.

It was night now, and a few feet beyond the ambulance a portable generator putted noisily. A bank of floodlights sent their beams stabbing through the darkness, highlighting portions of the bombed houseboat in harsh white and stark black. The shouts of the workers drifted across the water as they climbed around the wreckage looking for more survivors.

Several hundred Vietnamese onlookers had been drawn to the scene, and they stood around watching and eating pieces of fresh pineapple and dried squid. The vendors of these delicacies were enjoying a boom business as they circulated through the crowd selling their goods.

"Colonel Barclay?" a voice called, and Justin saw an

American officer, looking strangely out of place with his clean, crisp uniform.

"Yes," Justin replied, draining the rest of his coffee and stepping over to the American.

"Sir, General McKenzie sends his congratulations on the good work you are doing here, and asks if you would meet with him sometime tomorrow."

"Oh, that's right," Justin said suddenly. "I had forgotten all about General McKenzie. He wanted to see me today. Well, I'm through here, I could see him tonight if he wants."

"The General isn't seeing anyone tonight, sir," the young officer replied. "His son-in-law was killed in this explosion."

"Oh?" Justin said, "That's right—I'd forgotten Lieutenant Kaplan was his son-in-law. I'll see him tomorrow, then. Thank you for the message."

As the American officer left, one of the rescue workers told Justin that they had moved the last of the wreckage and there was no one still trapped. Justin thanked him and spoke with the remaining Vietnamese workers before he left to go home. It had been a long day, and he was glad it was over.

As Justin drove down Rue de Pasteur, the avenue of well-kept lawns and stately villas, occupied for the most part by the high-ranking military and government officials of Vietnam, he decided to stop at Doung's house. He would see how they were, make sure they hadn't been injured by the bomb blast.

Le greeted him, apologizing in front of the servants for the fact that her husband wasn't home.

'Where is he?" Justin asked, curious over his absence.

"He's trying to locate the terrorist who threw the bomb," Le said.

"Yes, he would be," Justin mused. "I can imagine that immediate revenge would be more important to the Saigon government than the rescue of the victims of the attack."

"How many were killed?" Le asked.

"Six—five Vietnamese and one American. Seven more were injured and trapped by the debris. We just got the last one out a short time ago."

"Oh, Justin, I wish I could leave this place. The violence, the terror. It is an evil place."

"There are no evil places, Le," Justin said. "Only evil people."

"Like my husband," Le replied quietly. Justin didn't answer.

THE RAINY SEASON was in full force, and that night as Justin waited on the balcony of the apartment he had rented, he watched the rain move off the Saigon River and slash across the roofs of the city. In the alley alongside the apartment two children sought shelter beneath a piece of corrugated tin, which they held over them. A bicyclist, pedaling through the rain furiously, flipped over on the slickened road and slid into a stack of two-gallon tin containers that had been carefully displayed by a sidewalk shopkeeper. The unfortunate bicyclist limped off with bleeding legs and a damaged bike, followed by the curses of outrage from the peddler.

The rain was also falling on Justin, and his uniform hung heavy with water, but he made no attempt to escape. He loved the rain. It blanketed all sight and sound and formed a curtain behind which his soul could exist in absolute solitude. Only those with whom he really wanted to share could penetrate it.

He thought of what he had told Le. There are no evil places, just evil people. Le had responded, "Like my husband."

But, was it only Duong, Nhu, and Diem? Could it be that some of the Americans, though with good intentions, were just as disruptive, if not evil?

WHEN JUSTIN REPORTED to General McKenzie the next day, he extended his sympathies on the death of Lieutenant Kaplan.

"Yes," McKenzie said without emotion. "It was a tragic thing. Still, such things happen in war, and a professional soldier must be able to adjust."

McKenzie started the elaborate procedure of filling his pipe, and he pointed to a chair, indicating that Justin should have a seat. Finally, he peered through a cloud of aromatic smoke and asked Justin, "Have you been briefed on Operation Valkyrie?"

"Valkyrie?" Justin replied. "No, sir. I don't think so."

"Read this," McKenzie said, sliding a folder across the top of his desk. The folder had a red border and was marked TOP SECRET.

The security classification surprised Justin, and he picked up the document a little hesitantly. He always felt conflicting emotions when dealing with top-secret material. On the one hand, there was the curiosity and excitement of the unknown. On the other, the knowledge that he was about to be made privy to information that by its very classification could result in "grave and perilous danger to the United States, as a result of unauthorized leakage" was intimidating. As such, he would be suspect, should the material be compromised.

"Go ahead, read it," McKenzie said as he saw Justin

hesitate over the classification. "You have a top-secret clearance, and in this case a bona fide need-to-know."

The document Justin read was the same cable that had been dispatched to the American Embassy the day before, with a few additional comments added by the SEAOP staff in Washington.

"That's Valkyrie," McKenzie said. He chuckled once. "It's quite a coincidence, of course, but it just so happens that 'Valkyrie' was also the code name for the attempted overthrow of Hitler in the generals' plot of 1944."

Justin put the document back in the security folder, and then placed the folder on the desk in front of General McKenzie.

"You said I have a bona fide need-to-know," Justin said. "Where do I fit in?"

"Right in the middle," McKenzie said. "In fact, you will be the middleman. No one knows the Vietnamese better than you. There is no one they would trust more than you. And, of course, we can't afford to do this openly. The entire operation has to be clandestine."

"I see," Justin said. "And you want me to find your plotters for you?"

"Oh, no," McKenzie said, smiling. "I've already found them. You need merely act as liaison for us."

"Who will I be seeing?"

"Well, on the American side you'll be working with Colonel Rogers," General McKenzie said. "And the leader of the coup element for the Vietnamese Army is General Le Van Tung.

"Tung!"

"Yes," McKenzie said, a small smile of intrigue playing across his lips. "Surprising, isn't it?"

"But Tung could never do it," Justin said. "He has no

support among the other army generals. He could never lead a coup. Where did you get such an idea?"

"From General Tung himself," McKenzie said triumphantly. "He came here, to my quarters, late at night. He asked for American support, and he said he represented several others."

"I—" Justin rubbed the back of his fist against his forehead as if trying to adjust to the shock of imagining Tung involved in a coup plot. "I don't doubt that Tung came to see you with such a request, General," Justin said, "but I would recommend that we not deal with Tung."

"I'm afraid that your recommendation has come too late," McKenzie replied shortly. "The decision has already been made. And it is irreversible. We will deal with General Tung!"

Justin knew it was useless to argue with the General. McKenzie was adamant.

There was a strained silence. Finally, McKenzie spoke again.

"Let me ask you something, Colonel Barclay. Do you believe a coup against Diem is inevitable?"

"Unless Diem changes drastically, and gets rid of the Nhus, then, yes, I believe there will be a coup," Justin agreed.

"Do you believe Diem will get rid of the Nhus?"

"No," Justin said quietly.

"Then, don't you think that with our help a coup would have a better chance of success? And that it could be accomplished with less bloodshed?"

"Yes," Justin agreed again.

"Then, I don't understand. What is your problem?" General McKenzie asked, folding his hands and leaning across his desk.

"My problem is not with the idea of a coup. Hell, that is historically the only way these people have of changing governments. It's just that I feel we ought to examine all the coup elements," Justin said. "Then we could decide which coup had the greatest chance of success, and which one would be the best for the Vietnamese people. And then we could back them."

"Even if I agreed with you in principle, I couldn't agree with you in operation," McKenzie replied. "Colonel, you must realize that we can't conduct this coup like a lottery, putting numbers into a hat, and then drawing some lucky General's name. We must remain in the background, and we must move quickly. General Tung obviously has a well-organized operation under way. He was the first one far enough along in his plans to seek our support. And the decision has been made to give him the support he needs."

"General, could I have just twelve hours to find a more suitable candidate?" Justin asked.

"No," General McKenzie said, definitely. "You will go with what we have. Colonel Barclay, if you feel that your support of Valkyrie isn't going to be enthusiastic, then I'd rather not use you at all. I'll use Colonel Rogers."

"How could you use him? He doesn't speak Vietnamese."

"His interpreter does, and he has an excellent rapport with his interpreter."

Justin thought about the problem for a few moments while McKenzie sat back in his chair, smoking his pipe in quietly audible puffs. Justin turned the problem in his mind, examining it like a diamond, looking at every facet. Tung's disgrace and sudden willingness to help seemed almost too convenient, Justin thought. If he did not agree to help, and McKenzie did go with Rogers,

Rogers would be totally unable to foresee any danger in the situation. If Tung did turn out to be loyal to Diem, and was merely testing the United States, then Rogers would fall right into Tung's trap. If Tung actually intended to attempt a coup, but without sufficient backing from his own people, Rogers would be unable to realize it in time. Either way it could be disastrous for America. On the other hand, if he did agree to help, he would be able to gauge Tung's true intentions and strength. Perhaps he could fend off a disaster before it occurred. And he would be in a position to find a legitimate coup element to contact.

"Well?" McKenzie asked quietly.

"I'll do it," Justin said.

McKenzie grinned broadly and reached out to shake Justin's hand. "I was hoping you would make that decision."

"Should I keep the assignment with the Special Police?" Justin asked.

"Yes, of course. We don't want to arouse any suspicion. Besides, you are in the best position to keep an eye on what's going on. Go on back now and get in touch with General Tung. Tell him that the United States is fully committed to support of the coup. Find out exactly what he wants, and tell him we'll supply it. Tell him that you are to be his only contact. Under no circumstances will any other American official get directly involved. You will be working very closely with Colonel Rogers. I've placed this under his psy-war section, and he'll make his facilities available to you."

## 11

Justin left General McKenzie's office and decided to drive the few blocks to the psy-war headquarters to talk with Colonel Rogers. He had never seen the psy-war operation. Now that he would be working with them, he thought it was about time he took a look at it.

Psy-war was situated in a small building sandwiched between a peasant's sidewalk restaurant and a small furniture shop. The pungent odor of *nuk mam* permeated the area around the small cafe. Shavings of wood from the furniture shop covered the sidewalk and crunched beneath Justin's feet as he entered the psy-war building.

Inside, the Vietnamese employees of the psy-war section were scurrying around, chattering noisily. Justin could hear the printing press as it turned out leaflets, and he saw newly printed stacks piled high on the tables along the walls. Women and children were putting the stacks into bundles and tying them up with string. Over in the corner, all alone, an old man squatted on the floor, making a drawing with a brush and India ink. The drawing would later be transferred to a leaflet for distribution.

Justin was greeted by an American sergeant. He was chewing a cigar, and wiping ink from his hands with a rag that merely spread the ink around but didn't remove it.

"Where is Colonel Rogers?" Justin asked.

The sergeant pulled the short cigar butt from his mouth and spat out a piece of it before he answered. "The Colonel don't never come down here."

"Isn't this psy-war headquarters?" Justin asked.

"It's where we do the work," the sergeant replied. "But the Colonel's office is over at MACV."

"Oh, I see," Justin said. He looked around the building. "You look busy."

"Colonel Rogers wanted us to meet the quota by the end of the day. He's comin' up with a new leaflet, and we gotta get these old ones out."

"Did you say 'quota'?"

"Yes, sir," the sergeant answered, sticking the cigar butt back in his mouth. "We were supposed to have 'til the thirtieth, but now we've got to get them out today, 'n it's only the twenty-sixth. Say, would you like a cook's tour of the shop? I can show you the operation 'bout as good as Colonel Rogers."

"Well, yes, if you don't mind," Justin said. "I'd like to take a look around."

The sergeant took Justin through the building, showing him the entire operation. He concluded by pulling out briefing charts indicating the number of leaflets printed and delivered each month. There was also a map of South Vietnam with various areas shaded in different colors. The sergeant explained that each color indicated the degree of saturation, and that the amount of saturation was linked to the suspected amount of Communist control of the area.

"Is this the same lecture everyone gets?" Justin asked.

"Sir, this is identical to what the Colonel gives the ambassador, visitin' generals, congressmen, and senators," the sergeant said proudly. "Colonel Rogers, he worked it out, 'n I put it on the charts for him. It's a means of judgin' how much good we're doin' and puttin' it on a percentage basis. Otherwise, there's no way to tell."

"But what is the basis of your figures?" Justin asked. "This isn't something you can put numbers to."

The sergeant looked at his briefing charts in confusion.

"I don't know nothin' about that," he finally said. "Colonel Rogers gets the figures somewhere. Like I said, I just put 'em down on the charts."

"What do the leaflets say?" Justin asked.

The sergeant pulled out an English version and handed it to Justin.

"Let me see one written in Vietnamese," Justin requested.

"You mean you can read that shit?" the sergeant asked in fascination.

"Yes," Justin replied, taking the Vietnamese leaflet. It was identical with the leaflet the villager in Hoa Ginh had shown him.

"Let me see the English version," he said.

He took the English translation from the sergeant and read it, and he felt the anger growing in him. "Is this supposed to say this?" he asked, holding the Vietnamese leaflet alongside the English translation.

"Why, yes, sir," the sergeant answered, confused by Justin's attitude. "Don't it?"

"No, sergeant," Justin said. "They don't say the same thing. What you are passing out has an entirely different meaning than was intended by the English version."

The sergeant looked at the two documents dumbly.

"I'm going to see Colonel Rogers," Justin said. "I'd suggest you not send any more of these out."

"But my quota," the sergeant insisted, spraying out pieces of his cigar as he protested.

"Goddammit, sergeant, can't you get it through your head that these leaflets are bad? Forget the quota until we get this straightened out."

Justin left the sergeant still scratching his head and drove over to MACV headquarters to see Colonel Rogers.

When he went into Colonel Rogers' office the Colonel and his interpreter were both waiting for him. Rogers was holding a copy of the English translation, and one of the leaflets that were being circulated. His eyes flashed angrily.

"My sergeant just called me," Rogers said. "What do you mean, ordering him to hold back on the leaflets? You have no authority in the psy-war department."

"Colonel Rogers, I'm sure you don't want to circulate these leaflets," Justin said calmly. "They are poorly translated, and they are creating the worst possible image for America."

"You're wrong," Colonel Rogers answered. "I have Mr. Mot here. He assures me that the translation is correct."

"The translation is not 'correct'," Justin said to Mot. "You have implied that—"

"Implied, Colonel?" Rogers asked, quickly interrupting Justin.

"Yes," Justin said.

"Colonel Barclay," Rogers said disgustedly, "I thought it might be something like this. I want you to know that I'm not interested in what you consider to be subtle implication. I want to know if the translation is accurate in actual meaning."

"There are meanings, and meanings, of words," Justin said.

"Colonel Barclay," Mot said in perfect English. He had practically no accent, but his voice carried an oily tone of patronization, which grated on Justin's nerves. "I greatly admire your mastery of our language. However, like a great many Westerners who have learned our language, you tend to read into it nuances that are not there. Perhaps you are overreacting to the 'inscrutable Oriental' syndrome. Nonetheless, I ask you to consider the message word for word and locate, if you can, an error."

"On a strict word-for-word translation, I doubt that I can find any errors," Justin said. "But in the phrasing—"

"Colonel Barclay," Rogers interrupted, "may I suggest that the phrasing is my job? Now, I have ordered the leaflets circulated, and I have reported your action to General McKenzie. He has instructed me to tell you that you are not to enter the psy-war building to interfere with its operation in any way. If you wish, he'll be glad to see you and pass that message on personally."

"Rogers, you are a damned fool," Justin said in resignation. "You are so afraid that I'm after your job. My only intention was to help you."

"I don't want your help," Colonel Rogers said shortly. "However, my orders are to work with you on Valkyrie. So, please confine your 'help' to that effort."

When Justin left MACV a few minutes later a boiling sea of frustrated rage churned his insides. The frustration was further aggravated by the traffic conditions he encountered as he drove back to the office he shared with Colonel Doung. The traffic was bad because it had been rerouted to avoid the ever-increasing student riots that were erupting throughout the city.

Despite the rerouted traffic, Justin's path caused him to skirt the edges of the disturbance. He caught several whiffs of tear gas, and he could hear the flat thump of gunfire as more gas canisters were shot into the crowds.

Suddenly several students ran from a nearby alleyway and charged Justin's Jeep. Because of Justin's job as advisor, his Jeep bore the coloring and markings of the Special Police, and that incensed the crowd.

"Go away, American pig!" they yelled, spitting at the Jeep. *"Di di My con heo!"* is the way it came out in Vietnamese.

One of the students picked up a rock and smashed Justin's windshield. Justin covered his face with his arm to protect it from flying glass and stepped on the accelerator, hoping he wouldn't hit anything as he left. One of the students grabbed the side of the Jeep and tried to hang on, spitting in Justin's face. Finally, he let go, and as Justin sped down the street he could see the student bouncing and sliding along the pavement behind his Jeep.

Suddenly, with an insight born of frustration and nurtured by fear, Justin was able to equate his plight with that of the young student who lay hurt and bleeding in the road behind him. He was being pulled along by events, and he could neither hang on nor let go.

JUSTIN RECEIVED A NOTE FROM GENERAL TUNG SETTING the time they would meet. Justin had thought it would be in one of the restaurants, but General Trans note had been very secretive, and promised that the address would be delivered later in a separate note. Justin thought that Tung's behavior was overly dramatic, but if he was to meet with Tung, he had no choice. He had to bow to Tung's wishes, melodramatic though they might be.

The address that Tung had finally given him was of a store that sold wicker baskets and earthenware pots. An old man, clacking an abacus, looked up as Justin entered. He didn't speak, but pointed with a bony finger to the back of the room. Justin went through a bead curtain, across a yard with an open cistern, and down an alley that stank of rotten vegetables. He had to climb a flight of rickety stairs to a small room. Inside, an old woman motioned for Justin to sit at a crude table, and she set a bottle of warm "33" beer in front of him.

A few moments later General Tung, again dressed in

nondescript civilian clothes, came into the room. The butt of a cigarette burned close to his lips. The very strong smell of the cheap Asian tobacco was heavy and oppressive in the close room.

"We will speak in French," Tung said.

"If you wish," Justin replied.

Tung lit a new cigarette from his old one before speaking again. "Will the Americans help me?"

"We are interested in bringing about a stabilized government. One that will serve the best interests of the Vietnamese people," Justin said.

"And you agree that Diem can't do this?" Tung asked.

"Why are you interested in overthrowing Diem?" Justin asked. "I thought you owed him a great deal. Isn't this a disloyal act?"

"My loyalty is to my country, not to Diem," Tung said.

"Quite frankly, General Tung," Justin replied, "your actions in the past have not always reflected that. You have endorsed Diem's Buddhist policy. What makes you think you could win the backing of the people?"

Tung's eyes flashed angrily. "Why do you question me? Why do you question my motives? There is only one question to be answered here. Will the Americans help?"

"What do you need?" Justin asked, being careful not to push Tung too far.

"How far will the Americans go?" Tung asked. "Will you help us fight against the troops that will be loyal?"

Justin had not discussed this aspect with McKenzie, but he was sure that it was further than the United States would want to go.

"You won't be able to count on us for armed support during the coup," Justin said. "But after the coup, if it is successful, we will aid in maintaining order."

"Will you give us direct support?" Tung asked. "Will

you provide us with transportation and communication facilities?"

"We will not withhold material that is already committed to the army," Justin said, "nor will we place any restrictions on how it is to be used."

"And now, Colonel Barclay, you will pardon the bluntness of this question, but you can understand I must ask it. You are but a Colonel. What proof do I have that you speak for the United States government, and not just for yourself, or for your General McKenzie?"

"You have my word as an officer," Justin said.

Tung laughed, and his breath was as foul as his teeth were ugly. "I'm afraid that isn't enough. I need evidence of your good faith and of your authority."

Justin looked at the bottle of beer on the table in front of him and smiled. "Listen to the Voice of America broadcast tomorrow night. I will have them include the message 'The beer is warm.'" Justin said the phrase in English. "That should show that I have the authority of the government behind me."

"Yes," Tung said, laughing again. "Yes. I will listen. If I hear the message, I will know that the United States is committed to the coup."

"What are your plans?" Justin asked. "And what support do you have?"

General Tung stood to leave. "I won't speak of this now," he said. "If I hear your message over the Voice of America broadcast tomorrow night, then we will meet again in two days."

"Very well," Justin said. He was disgusted with himself. He had been so confident that he would be able to conduct the negotiations better than Colonel Rogers, and avoid Tung's cunning. But in this first exchange, Tung had clearly gotten the best of him. Tung would have proof of official United States intentions without having disclosed any of his own plans. Justin had lost the first move.

When Justin returned to his office Colonel Doung was standing at the door talking with one of the other officers. He smiled broadly when he saw Justin.

"Ah, here you are. I was just leaving a message for you. I have some entertainment planned. I'm sure you will enjoy it."

"Entertainment?" Justin asked. "What type of entertainment?"

"Oh, come, come. It's very rude to question the plans of your host. Come with me and see for yourself. I assure you, you will find it interesting."

Justin rode in the Jeep with Colonel Doung down Ben Chuoung Duong Street until they came to the mass of open marketplaces that dealt primarily with the Vietnamese. The merchants here were not the black marketeers of the type prevalent on Tu Do Street. Instead, they were following the customs of hundreds of years. Jabbering little Vietnamese women sifted through the markets, here buying a fish, there a head of cabbage, as they did their shopping.

Colonel Doung stopped the Jeep in a no-parking zone, and they walked over to the edge of the market, where they stood for a few seconds. An old woman was sitting on the sidewalk at their feet plucking fleas from the head of a little boy, who looked up at Justin. His face was encrusted with mucus from his nose and drainage from open sores. He held his hand out, palm up, wordlessly asking for money.

Colonel Doung looked at his watch impatiently, and with that gesture clearly pointed out the gulf separating him from his fellow countrymen who milled about him.

For the average Vietnamese, there are only two times: daytime or nighttime.

"Ah, here they are," Doung said, smiling.

A two-and-one-half-ton truck braked to a stop, and two armed men jumped down from the back and looked up at the truck, their weapons at the ready. A man looked out of the back of the truck, terror clearly marked in his face, then disappeared into the darkened interior. He reminded Justin of an animal in a zoo who would take a quick peek at the people and then retreat to the back of his cage to try to avoid them.

A Jeep pulled up alongside the truck, mounting a 50-caliber machine gun. There was some yelling, and four men finally emerged from the back of the truck, all of them as frightened and as confused as the one whose face Justin had glimpsed earlier.

"One of these young men threw the bomb at the My Kahn," Doung said.

"Which one?" Justin asked.

"We don't know, but they do. And that makes them all equally guilty. They also participated in the riots. They are students." Doung screwed his face into a derisive expression as he said the word, setting it apart from the rest of the sentence and flavoring it with repugnance.

"I don' t understand," Justin said. "Why are they here?"

"A public execution may discourage others from the same foolishness," Doung said.

"You are going to execute them right here, in the public square?" Justin asked. "That's the sort of thing I've been telling you about. How do you ever hope to win the support of the people in this way?"

"I don't need their support," Doung said, taking in the people of the market with a wave of his hand. "All I need is their fear. And for that a public execution is the best method."

The guards moved the four men into position against the wall of one of the nearby buildings. The bolt on the Jeep-mounted machine gun was slammed home.

"My God, Doung," Justin gasped, "you're not going to execute them with a fifty-caliber machine gun? Those rounds are damn near as big as a man's fist! They'll chop them up like ground meat."

"But their deaths will be sure," Doung said. Children, dirty, their skins covered with scabs and their hair full of lice, edged closer to the Jeep. They put their fingers in their ears and waited patiently to move in and strip the bodies as soon as the firing had stopped.

While Justin watched in disbelief and horror, the gun opened up, not popping like a small gun, but exploding in earth-shaking, stomach-jarring blasts.

The little men began to fly apart. Arms and legs were literally cut away. One of them was completely cut in half. The top of his body toppled over backward, and the bottom half stood for a moment gushing blood, then fell forward.

Suddenly the gun stopped, and the relative silence of bickering Vietnamese again filled the air. Only the children watched; the vendors and the buyers seemed oblivious to the killings.

Justin stood there for several seconds fighting the nausea. Doung pulled a silk handkerchief from his pocket and wiped his hands vigorously. His eyes had a demonic glow.

"I thought that since you were directly involved with the bombing, you would be pleased to see that justice was done," he said.

Justin couldn't speak. He was unable to force the words through the grim shock he felt.

"Well," Doung said, seeing how Justin was reacting, "perhaps I misjudged your threshold of sensitivity. We'll go now. I have something arranged that I'm sure you will enjoy."

Justin followed Doung, but it was almost by reflex. He was anxious to get away from the scene of horror, where the children were now fighting with one another for possession of the clothes the prisoners had been wearing. He looked away as they drove off, and breathed deeply to fight the nausea.

"I'm sorry that you weren't entertained," Doung said, as if apologizing for a bad choice in recommending a movie to a friend. "I suppose I tend to forget that not everyone shares my lust for blood. But for me, there is something very exciting about the sudden death of an enemy."

"You aren't saying that just to shock me, are you?" Justin asked. "You really mean it."

"Yes, yes, I mean it." Doung laughed. "It even gets me sexually excited. Explain that to me, if you can."

"I'm afraid I can't," Justin replied.

The Jeep stopped in front of a building in Cholon. There was a large wall around the building and a private guard standing by the gate.

"What is this place?" Justin asked.

"I promised you some entertainment, and now I'm going to deliver. You didn't like the other, but I know you'll like this," Doung replied. "Come, we'll go inside."

The grounds inside the walls were laid out in a Japanese garden. Box hedges, tiny, beautifully trimmed trees, and a red and gold bridge arching gracefully over a quiet pool made the scene like something out of

Madame Butterfly. An old woman handed them each a kimono and a towel and directed them toward a room, where they were met by two beautiful women who indicated that they were there to bathe them.

"I thought you might enjoy this," Doung said as he settled down into his bathtub. There was a bamboo screen separating his bathtub from the one used by Justin, so that they couldn't see each other, but they could talk.

"This is more to my liking," Justin agreed. The bath was sensual and relaxing. The girl assigned to him was beautiful, and she was wearing only panties and a brassiere, but Justin intuitively knew that she was not a prostitute and he was glad.

After the bath Justin wrapped himself in a large towel and went into a small room that opened just off the big bathroom. There was a bed in the room, and a small electric fan played a cool breeze across the bed.

Justin put on the comfortable kimono and then lay down on the bed. He closed his eyes to luxuriate in the total comfort, and had almost gone to sleep when he was roused by a gentle voice.

"Colonel Doung has sent me to you. I hope I am worthy."

Justin opened his eyes in surprise and looked at the girl standing by his bed. She was totally nude, and her skin was beautiful and without blemish. She was nearly without curves as well, having only tiny suggestions or breasts. The girl could not have been over twelve-years-old.

"What?" Justin asked.

"I am here to make love to you," the girl said with a shy smile. "I hope you find me pleasing."

"No!" Justin protested.

Tears sprang to the young girl's eyes. "You find me ugly?"

"*Em* ah," Justin said, using the Vietnamese term of affection, "Colonel Doung has played a trick on you. I think you are very pretty—but I cannot do it."

"It won't work?" the girl asked, pointing toward Justin s groin, her face registering sympathy for him.

"That's right," Justin said, deciding it was easier to let the girl believe that. "It's not your fault. Colonel Doung doesn't have to find out."

If Justin had not been fully committed to Valkyrie before, he was now. But Diem and Nhu were only incidental to the operation. His real goal now was to get Colonel Doung out of power. Even if it meant killing him.

## 13

On the seventh of September, it rained in Saigon. Not a hard, cleansing rain, but a soft spray, which carried trapped within its fine mist some of the ash from the sections of the city the students had burned. For two weeks now the students had carried their demonstrations against the government out of the schools and into the streets. Fires, looting, and shooting were nightly occurrences.

The gray light of morning disclosed piles of rubble and charred, smoking timbers. Where fires still smoldered, the falling rain hissed and popped like the sputtering fuse of a live hand grenade. Scattered pockets of tear gas hung in visible clouds, and became such a constant reality that the people walked the streets with handkerchiefs clutched against nose and mouth.

A small bit of bread, wet and sodden, lay in a gutter of black rushing water in front of a burned-out bicycle shop on Le Loi. A rat, beady eyes alert for danger, darted out to the prize, grabbed it, and bounded back to the comparative safety of the destroyed building.

Only two short blocks away in actual distance, but a world away in fact, Antoine Mouchette sat at his breakfast table. It was covered with a white linen cloth and set with sparkling white china, glistening crystal, and highly polished silver. A uniformed domestique hovered close by, ready to attend to the slightest wish of Mouchette or his guest. This morning his guest was General Le Van Tung.

General Tung pulled out a crumpled package for a cigarette, but it was empty. Mouchette snapped his fingers, and a silver cigarette box appeared almost instantly. Tung took several, poking the ones he didn't smoke into his crumpled pack. Mouchette smiled but said nothing.

"So," Tung said after his cigarette was lit, "the Americans are prepared to sponsor a coup."

"You are sure of this?" Mouchette asked.

The cigarette Tung was smoking was American, and Tung held the smoke for several seconds, enjoying the unfamiliar mildness. Finally, he let it escape with a contented sigh and answered. "Yes. We asked for a key message to be sent over VOA, and it was. That confirms that our contact is indeed working with American blessing."

Mouchette took a bite of his breakfast melon and looked at General Tung. He didn't speak, because he wanted to be sure of exactly what Tung wanted of him first, and even an inflection of the voice could prematurely commit his position.

"I am their contact and will be organizing the coup," Tung said. He smiled and flicked a piece of tobacco off his lip with his tongue before he went on. "With President Diem's backing, of course," he added with a thin laugh. "The Americans are such fools."

Mouchette could breathe more easily now. He knew where Tung stood and could act accordingly. "And you want my assistance?"

"Monsieur Mouchette. I am sure that you recognize the debt you owe our government. We could have undertaken nationalization proceedings against your holdings long ago. However, due to the mutual respect and friendship you enjoy with our leaders, we did not," Tung said.

"Respect perhaps, but more nearly correct is the fact that you would lose a great sum of money if you were to do such a thing," Mouchette said easily. "My taxes and bribe money would stop, and there are a large number of people in high government places who wouldn't like that."

"It isn't bribe money, Monsieur Mouchette. It is the ancient and honored Asian tradition of *cumshaw—* money paid as a gratuity for special services rendered. And you must admit that there have been special services."

Mouchette thought of the laws that had been passed virtually assuring him a monopoly in the rubber production of the country. There were also other benefits, such as free labor from the prisons and official government sanctions of practices which gave his international wheeling and dealing a modicum of legality, if not respectability.

Mouchette returned General Tung's smile. "We have both profited by our association, I agree. Now, how may I be of help?"

"I understand you have social contact with General McKenzie and other highly placed American officials," General Tung said. He lit a new cigarette from his old one, pinched the fire off the end of the old one with yellowed fingers, and then pocketed the butt.

"Yes," Mouchette answered. He had picked up an ashtray to offer General Tung, but put it down quickly.

"Have you a method of influencing him?"

"Do you mean blackmail?"

"Something a bit more subtle," General Tung suggested.

At that moment, Mouchette's mistress, Tamara. walked into the dining room carrying a bouquet of flowers she had just picked in the garden. Droplets of water clung to the petals of the flowers. They also nestled in her hair, where each one acted as a tiny prism and flashed its colors like brilliant jewels. She smiled at Mouchette and Tung, then began to arrange the flowers in a beautiful vase of intricate design from the Ming dynasty.

"Yes, I think I may have the *levier de commanded*," Mouchette said, looking at Tamara. "What do you want me to do?"

"I want you to make sure that the United States commits itself to me only. They must not be receptive to any other coup proposals."

"That should be an easy enough task," Mouchette said. "You may count on my assistance."

"Mr. Nhu said as much," Tung said. "He is aware of your patriotism."

Mouchette smiled wryly. "You may tell Mr. Nhu for me that my concern for the welfare of the people of Vietnam is equaled only by his own."

"Excellent," Tung said. He looked around the room as if trying to find his hat, but one of the servants, anticipating him, had already retrieved it. He handed the hat to Tung, and then waited quietly to escort him from the house.

General Tung saluted Mouchette, made a half bow toward Tamara, and then followed the servant out.

"Antoine, why do you get involved?" Tamara asked as she continued to work with the flowers. "You owe no allegiance to the Diem government. If you play in the water, you are going to get wet."

"I owe allegiance only to Antoine Mouchette," Mouchette said. "And I remain above their politics like an oil slick on water. I will ride with the tides and conform to the shape of things, but I won't get involved and I won't get wet. I think it temporarily serves my best interests to cooperate with Diem—or at least to give that illusion. But do not distress yourself. I intend to leave all the other options open."

Tamara selected one of the flowers and brought it over to Mouchette. She stuck it in his lapel, then looked at him and smiled. "That's what I love about you, Antoine. You are so evil." She pulled his face down to hers and kissed him deeply.

"Don't waste all that on me," Mouchette said, pushing her away gently. "General McKenzie will be here this morning. And it is very important that we get him in a good mood."

"General McKenzie is a dirty old man," Tamara said, pouting. "I don't like being with him. He sweats."

Mouchette kissed Tamara on the forehead and then took her chin between his thumb and forefinger. "Be good to him for me."

"If I'm good to him, will you be good to me?" Tamara asked coyly.

Mouchette pulled her against him. "I'm always good," he said.

. . .

THE RAIN, which only served to make the rest of the city look dirty, caused the well-scrubbed Mouchette estate to sparkle, and as General McKenzie looked through the back window of Mouchette's Mercedes he felt a twinge of envy for the wealth that could create such a garden in the midst of a cesspool. But he hadn't come here to admire the landscape. He had come here to visit Princess Tamara, as he had on every opportunity since he first met her.

"Ah, General McKenzie, how nice of you to call on me," Mouchette said by way of greeting. "Come in, come in. What brings you?"

"I—uh, thought I'd stop by and see if any of the unpleasantness has disturbed you," McKenzie said.

"Unpleasantness?" Mouchette asked, raising his eyebrows in question.

"Yes, the student riots," McKenzie replied, gesturing with his hands as if to call Mouchette's attention to the fact that there was another world outside.

"Oh," Mouchette said, smiling. "I hadn't really given them a thought. By the way, just for you I've acquired some coffee. Perhaps you'd like some, with a few *tourteaux*?"

McKenzie looked around the room, seemingly oblivious to Mouchette's question. Mouchette laughed.

"I meant later, of course," he said.

"I beg your pardon?" McKenzie asked, only now aware that Mouchette had spoken.

Mouchette pointed toward a door. "I know," he said patronizingly. "You wish to see Tamara. She saw you drive up and wishes to see you in there. Perhaps afterward you'll take coffee with me, and we can chat?"

"Yes, I'd like that," McKenzie said. But he started for the door before Mouchette could answer him, his eyes already taking on a glow of anticipation.

WHEN MCKENZIE EMERGED over an hour later, Mouchette was sitting behind the table reading a newspaper. McKenzie sat in a chair near the table, and a servant appeared with a lemon-scented, dampened towel. General McKenzie held it against his sweating face, grateful for its coolness but embarrassed by the fact that his recent sexual activity was common knowledge. He avoided the servant's eyes, even though they were expressionless. I'm a general, McKenzie thought. I'm not a private in the rear-assed ranks. I needn't feel like I've come to a whorehouse. That girl in there, why, she's a princess, a real princess—and you certainly wouldn't find a princess in a whorehouse. So why should I feel embarrassed?

The servant withdrew, and General McKenzie remained quiet for a few moments more.

As if giving McKenzie time to be with his own thoughts, Mouchette read the paper in silence. After a while he folded it and put it aside.

"The princess certainly looks forward to your visits," he said.

"She is very beautiful," McKenzie replied, not knowing what else to say.

"Well, now for our chat," Mouchette said. He leaned across the table and spoke quietly, as if drawing McKenzie into a conspiracy. "I know that the Americans have grown tired of Diem's government and wish to install a new one."

"What?" McKenzie asked, clearly startled. "Why would you say such a thing?"

"I am right, am I not?" Mouchette questioned. "The United States has decided to back the coup plans of General Tung?"

McKenzie stared at Mouchette in total shock. His mouth was open, and he was unable to speak.

"Oh, don't be so alarmed. It isn't common knowledge. It just so happens that I have my own system for finding out things. But I must say that this information came from a high, unimpeachable source, as your American newspapers sometimes say."

"I—I had no idea it would be compromised so quickly," McKenzie said, his voice colored with disappointment. "Naturally, the plan will have to be dropped."

"Don't be so hasty," Mouchette said. "Your choice of General Tung is a good one. Not too many know of the operation. Let it develop for a while. The secret is still safe."

"Do you know General Tung very well?" McKenzie asked, his eyes narrowing as he realized that he might be able to turn what had been a source of diversion into a source of information.

"I know Tung intimately," Mouchette said. "And I have known his family."

"You know, I had always figured Tung as one of Diem's staunchest yes-men," McKenzie said. "His plan for a coup surprised me, I must admit."

"Ah, but he is in disgrace, and an Oriental in disgrace lives only for revenge," Mouchette said. "You do well to back him."

McKenzie accepted the coffee that was handed him and took a swallow before he replied. "I'm awfully glad to hear you say that, Antoine. One of my officers, a

Colonel, feels that we are making a big mistake. I don't mind telling you that his opinion had me worried. He understands these people."

Mouchette smiled easily. "You are talking about Colonel Barclay, no doubt. I'll admit that Colonel Barclay is a rather amazing American, since he is so fluent in the language here. But don't confuse linguistic ability with political astuteness. Colonel Barclay is apt to be unduly influenced by some of his friends, who for personal ambitions would take the coup for themselves."

"Colonel Barclay feels that he could select a person more suited to our needs."

"General, don't forget that I am a third-generation Vietnamese, despite the fact that I also hold French citizenship. I know these people, and I know that some who have most influenced certain Americans, Colonel Barclay included, are nothing but opportunists."

"Monsieur Mouchette, I really don't have any right to ask this, but..." McKenzie began. He hesitated.

"Please, ask anything," Mouchette said. "I thought we had become good enough friends so that you wouldn't have to hesitate."

"I was wondering if I could count on you and your knowledge of these people? And of their language, of course, to, well, sort of monitor things, and keep me informed?"

"Of course, you can," Mouchette answered generously.

"I would find it an honor to help you."

"We have operatives—Vietnamese, you understand—whose job it is to do such things for us. But, frankly, I would tend to give your information a bit more credence, because you are, well, more like one of us—if you know what I mean?"

"I know exactly what you mean," Mouchette said easily. "And you are quite right. The Oriental is quite difficult to understand unless you have many years of experience. You can count on me."

McKenzie drained the last of his coffee, then looked at his watch. "I must be getting along. General Harkins is holding a briefing. We've got some visiting dignitaries coming—General Krulak from the Pentagon and Joseph Mendenhall from the State Department." McKenzie gave a derisive laugh. "They are 'fact-finders'—but of course, they will find only those facts we wish them to find."

Mouchette walked to the door with General McKenzie and saw him out. He had a difficult time containing his triumph until the General left. McKenzie couldn't have played more into his hands.

"Has he gone?" Tamara asked, and Mouchette saw her standing in the doorway that led to the bedroom she and McKenzie had used. She was wearing a hip-length peignoir, and her long, graceful legs glowed in the soft light.

"He's gone," Mouchette said.

## 14

PHU COUNG SITS ON A BEND IN THE RIVER ABOUT FIFTEEN miles north of Saigon. Phu Coung supplies fish to the markets of all nearby hamlets, and the fishmongers of the hamlets come to town every day to buy. They walk along the bank of the river and poke through the catch, which, when laid out, stretches for almost a quarter of a mile.

To the occasional visitor the smell is very strong. But, of course, the Phu Coung resident isn't aware of it. To him the fish market is an exciting place. It is the center of great activity. In addition to the customers and vendors, there are also the passengers of the bus line and the ferry service, both of which use the market as a terminal.

There are also many portable sidewalk cafes that are marvels of logistic ingenuity. Their owners, men and women alike, assemble the cafes every morning and disassemble them every night. They carry them about in two large boxes suspended from each end of a long pole, which they balance on their shoulders as they shuffle down the street. In one box, packed neatly, with every item exactly fitted into place like a ball within a ball within a ball, there are tables and chairs, and even the box, which becomes part of the counter. In the other box, utensils, spices, and other paraphernalia to stock the restaurant, and, of course, the box itself, to complete the counter. Within moments the sidewalk cafe can take on the appearance of a permanent fixture.

When a customer patronizes the cafe, the cafe owner-chef and his customer stroll through the quarter-mile-long display of fish until they select the one the customer wishes to eat. Then the haggle begins. Although the same people may have been doing business in the same location for forty years, they approach each new transaction as if for the first time.

"This is a fine fish," the restaurant patron will say, pointing to one.

The fish dealer will smile and nod enthusiastically. "You have chosen wisely. It is the best of all my fish and very fresh, only just caught and placed here."

"But I saw this same fish yesterday," the cafe owner complains.

"Not this fish. His brother, which I sold—and the customer returned to tell me it was the best fish he had ever eaten."

"The fish will be bony," the cafe owner warns.

The fish dealer picks up the fish and squeezes it. "You are *dingy-dau*! This fish has much sweet meat, very few bones."

"Oh, who am I to argue? It is for my customer," the cafe owner sighs. "He wants the fish, and I must please him. But I would never buy such a fish for myself. How much for him?"

"Forty dong," the fish dealer offers, his eyes narrowing, knowing his price is unreasonably high.

"Twenty."

"Thirty-five."

"Twenty-five."

"You take unfair advantage of me," the fish dealer complains. "You know I must sell him or lose him by spoilage. I lose money, but—thirty."

"The cost is so high I have no profit left for my cafe," the cafe owner complains. But he hands the money to the fish dealer, and indeed he has had the money in his hand all along, knowing full well what the settled price would be.

ON THE MORNING of September 9th, Justin sat at the counter of one of the Phu Coung cafes waiting for Le to return from the orphanage, which was close by. He had finished his meal and was drinking a bottle of beer and playing *co tuong* with an old man he had met there. *Co tuong* is a type of Asian chess. It has a few additional pieces and more complex moves than the chess of the Western world, but the basis is the same. It was unusual to see an American playing it, and amazing to see one playing it well, so several people had gathered around to watch.

Justin was beating the old man. It was a difficult moment, because to beat him would cause the old man great embarrassment. But to purposely lose to him would bring about dishonor, should it be discovered. So, the best course for Justin was to try to win. And it looked as if he was about to do just that.

The old man made a move, and Justin groaned inwardly. The decision point had arrived. He could move one piece, which would give the illusion of continuing the fight, but would in reality save the old man from harm over his move, or he could move another piece, which would take advantage of the old man's move and put the old man in an even worse position than he was in now. Justin decided to play to win, and he made the proper move.

"You are a very wise person," the old man said, smiling. "You could have carried me graciously, but I see you respect me and have made the proper move."

Justin was a little surprised. If the old man realized what he had done, why had he moved so?

"I wanted to judge your sincerity," the old man said, as if answering Justin's unasked question. "You will forgive a foolish old man for cloaking such curiosity in a game of *co tuong*?"

Then the old man made a move that changed the entire complexion of the game and elicited a gasp of surprise and admiration from Justin. It was a brilliant stroke.

"You are a master!" Justin said. "To have played that move you had to have several hundred possible sets in your mind at one time!"

"It is easy to keep such things in mind," the old man said, "as long as one follows order and form."

Justin tried to stave off defeat, but within a few moves he had lost the game.

"Thank you for the game, my young friend. You played well," the old man said.

Justin shook the old man's hand, and marveled again at his brilliance. "May I buy you a beer?" he asked.

"Yes, you may," the old man agreed. "I'm glad to see you like our game of *co tuong*."

"I like it very much. Do you like chess?" Justin asked.

The old man smiled. "Yes. I had some very good games of chess when I was in France many years ago.

My opponent honored me by allowing me to play with him. He was a master, and I was but an impudent pup. We played many games, and he beat me many times, but I was sometimes lucky and beat him."

"Who was the chess master?"

"A German, named Emanuel Lasker. He was an excellent player."

"I guess he was!" Justin exclaimed. "He was world's champion for over a quarter of a century."

As Justin and the old man finished their beer Le returned from the orphanage. She stopped a few feet away and looked at the ground.

"Oh," Justin said, seeing Le. "I would like you to meet someone, but I don't know your name."

"Nguyen," the old man said. He looked at Le quietly.

"This is Madam Doung," Justin said.

Le put the palms of her hands together and pointed the tips of the fingers down. It was a typical Oriental gesture, but rather unusual for Le. Justin was a little surprised by it.

"*Chow co, em*," Nguyen said. "I have had an interesting time with your American friend."

"He is the American advisor to my husband," Le replied in formal Vietnamese.

"Your husband is indeed a lucky man to receive advice from such a wise person."

"I am honored by your praise," Justin said.

"We must return now, Colonel Barclay," Le said. "Good day to you, Cao Ba Nguyen."

"Have a safe journey," Nguyen said.

"WHO IS THAT MAN?" Justin asked later as they were driving back to Saigon.

"An elder of the village," Le replied. It had been her first words since leaving.

"But you called him by his whole name."

"It would have been impolite of me to have done otherwise," Le said simply.

"But I didn't give you his whole name. I didn't even know it. You obviously know him."

"Everyone in Phu Coung knows him," Le said. "Why do you ask so many questions?"

"Le, why are you so upset? Is something wrong?"

"No—I—old men like that have powers. I didn't want his disapproval."

"I didn't know," Justin said. "I had no wish to make you uncomfortable."

Le smiled. "We will not talk of it. Did you have a good lunch?"

"Yes. And how was your visit to the orphanage?"

"My visit to the orphanage was good."

"I'm glad, but I have to get back now," Justin said, looking at his watch.

"I could tell Doung that I caused your delay," Le said.

Justin wasn't meeting Colonel Doung. He was meeting General Tung, and then, shortly after, Dương Văn Minh, or Big Minh, as General Minh was known. But he didn't tell that to Le.

"Thank you, but that won't be necessary."

WHEN THEY CROSSED THE RIVER, and were once again in Saigon, they felt the air was charged with a tension that was even greater than it had been for the last few weeks. All up and down both sides of the street people were walking and milling about and jabbering excitedly. It was especially noticeable because, despite the crowds, the markets were not doing business. Most of the vendors sat on their haunches chewing on the end of a stick that had been treated with betel nut and looking over the crowd dispassionately. Many of the other vendors had abandoned their wares entirely and stood in clusters along the edge of the street waiting expectantly.

One particularly unusual fact was that there was very little traffic on the streets. Even the cyclos, both the motor-driven and the pedal-type, were parked along the side of the street. Their drivers sat in the passenger seat, passing cigarettes back and forth, waiting along with everyone else.

As they approached Phu By Street and the large school they saw a burning Jeep, an overturned taxi, and several armed members of the Special Police. Justin pulled to the side of the road and stopped.

"What is it? What's going on?" Le asked.

"It looks as if the police are in the school there," Justin said, pointing down the road.

"But that is a school for children!" Le said. "It is what the Americans call an elementary school. Why would the police be here?"

"I don't know," Justin replied. "I think I'll find out, though. Look, perhaps you'd be better off not riding in this Jeep under the circumstances. Why don't you take a cyclo?"

"You will be careful?" Le asked anxiously as she stepped from the Jeep.

"Yes, of course," Justin replied.

Justin parked the Jeep near the school and walked onto the grounds. He had no trouble getting by the guards, because even those who didn't recognize him recognized the Vietnamese rank pinned to the pocket of his American uniform.

Behind the large brick and plaster wall that surrounded the school, in the courtyard, the place was in shambles. Broken glass, smashed desks, tables and chairs, and scattered books and papers were strewn about. At one side of the courtyard there appeared to be an interrogation area. Justin saw Colonel Doung, along with several other officers, talking with a group of Vietnamese—or rather, shouting at them. The Vietnamese were standing quietly, their heads bowed, listening to the abuse heaped on them by Doung. They were teachers from the school. Justin started toward them.

"Why are you here?" Doung asked rather sharply and in English. "I thought you were with my wife."

"We just got back," Justin said. "What is happening here?"

"It should be easy enough to see. The entire school system has been occupied by government forces. We've had to move to crush the rebellion."

"But this isn't a university!" Justin complained. "These kids are no older than twelve."

"Come with me," Doung ordered.

Justin followed Doung along the wall, by the side of the building, and into the back. A three-quarter-ton truck sat in the alleyway. Its tires were still burning, and the truck itself was a blackened hulk. Nothing was left of the steering wheel but a wire frame. The cushions were burned completely away, showing only the heat-rusted pattern of the seat springs.

"Two of my men were killed in this," Doung said. "A Molotov cocktail thrown by a ten-year-old girl."

"How are you so sure who threw it?"

Doung pulled out a handkerchief and wiped his hands before he answered. "Because we shot her," he said flatly. He pointed to a bamboo mat on the ground, and

Justin saw her for the first time. Actually, he could see only her legs as they protruded from beneath the mat. They were covered with scars from years of mosquito bites. One foot was bare. A tiny sandal dangled from the toe of the other foot, which was elevated slightly by a rock. A pool of red oozed through the weave of the mat.

"Were these the only casualties?" Justin asked.

"They were the only ones killed. There is an aid station inside the building for those who were injured. Everything is under control now. We will occupy the schools, we will occupy the pagodas, we will jail all troublemakers, and we will end this trouble," Doung said, almost as if making a speech.

"What happens when Diem runs out of jail space?" Justin asked.

"Simple," Doung answered flatly. "We'll kill enough prisoners to make room in the jails for more."

Justin returned to his Jeep so that he could keep his meeting with Tung, and later with Big Minh. A government sound truck was rolling slowly down the street playing music and making announcements concerning the National Assembly elections, which were to be held on September 27, having been postponed from August 31.

The words coming from the loudspeakers spoke of the peace and stability and progress toward prosperity which the people were enjoying under the Diem government, and urged continued support for it. The sound truck had to steer around the overturned taxi and the burned Jeep.

115

## 15

GENERAL TUNG HAD ASKED JUSTIN TO MEET HIM IN THE Cercle Sportif, where high-ranking American and Vietnamese officers met to play handball and tennis. The Cercle Sportif was also a popular place for the South Vietnamese legislators, who worked out in purple satin gym clothes while their chauffeurs kept the engines running in the air-conditioned Mercedes so the cars would be cool for their return.

Because of the nature of the place Justin was a little surprised that Tung had chosen it as their meeting spot.

"Who would ever suspect that such plans would be made here?" Tung asked, explaining his choice. He was dressed in tennis clothes, and he asked Justin to play a game with him to give credibility to their meeting. They played a few sets, then afterward sat in the folding chairs at the side of the court drinking from frosted glasses and watching a game being played on the far side of the court.

There were several moments of silence, interrupted

only by the hollow thunk of the tennis ball and the tinkling of the ice in the glasses they held.

Finally, Justin spoke. "The mood of the city worsens. Now the schools have been occupied by the police."

"It is a terrible thing for our country," Tung answered. "I am anxious to remove this yoke of oppression from them. It is for this reason that I intend to make the coup and no other. I have no personal ambitions."

Justin moved an ice cube around with his finger, then looked up at Tung, squinting in the bright sun. "When will you move?" Justin asked.

"We should not move too quickly," Tung said. "There are still important units that must be persuaded to join us. To move too quickly would jeopardize the entire operation."

"Have you organized a junta? Who are the officers involved?" Justin asked.

"We have not yet completed the organization," Tung said. "And there are some who still wish to be unknown. You will learn who they are in due time."

"General Tung, there are others who have approached us to seek our help. And I must confess that they appear to be better organized than you. They are prepared to apprise us of the makeup of their group and furnish us with specific plans and timetables. As you know, one of the conditions of our support is that we approve of the participants."

General Tung's eyes narrowed. "We cannot afford splinter elements now. If we are to succeed, we must be united behind a common effort. I'll make a proposal to you. In order that we may be united, suppose you prepare a list of names of officers from the other coup elements? Officers your country can trust. I'll take the list to my people, and using it, prepare a junta."

Justin was silent for a moment. Finally, he spoke quietly. "General Tung, you are asking me to assume a great risk for these men."

"Risks are taken in a war," Tung answered rather shortly. "Colonel, your country has taken the step to support a coup. You cannot escape with hands absolutely clean. You want approval of the ruling faction after the coup d'état. What better way than to provide us with the list of acceptable candidates?"

"I cannot act on this alone," Justin said. "I'll need to discuss it with my higher-up."

"To show you my good faith I will tell you what my plans are and give you my timetable," Tung said. "I plan to launch an all-out attack on Saigon for control of the government. I'm lining up units for my army, and I'll add the units of the commanders you give me. Against such a combined operation, the few troops who will be loyal to Diem will be helpless. I will start this action on the tenth day of October."

"I will contact my government," Justin said.

"I am sure General McKenzie will wish to cooperate," Tung said. "I don't imagine the American government is too pleased with our current 'school crisis.'"

Justin recalled the scene at the school, and his mouth drew into a tight line. "I'll be in touch," he promised.

Justin's second meeting of the day was with General Minh. The meeting with Big Minh had to be more secretive than the one with Tung. Not even the American government knew that Justin was dealing, surreptitiously with Big Minh.

Justin had met Big Minh ten years before, when Minh had been a major, fighting with the French against the Viet Minh. Justin had been assigned to the French as an observer, and his first action was the battle of Tu Ba. It was almost his last.

THE VIETNAMESE FIELD commanders had warned the French that Tu Ba could not be defended, and when Justin saw the report and called it to the attention of the French, they laughed and said that it was SOP for the Viets to report everything twice as bad as it really was. Since Justin was an observer, he decided to go to Tu Ba and observe.

"I am Big Minh," Minh said, introducing himself with a large grin when Justin reported to him at Tu Ba. Big Minh held out his hand, and Justin shook it, surprised at the size of the Vietnamese soldier before him. Big Minh was at least six feet tall, and weighed over two hundred pounds.

"Have you brought troops for us?" Minh asked.

"No," Justin said. "I have come to observe."

"You have come to die," Big Minh said matter-of-factly. "I am sorry, because this is not your war." Minh looked out across the river with his binoculars. "You still have time to go."

Justin looked around. "It looks as if you could use every man you could get. I'll stay."

"You are foolish," Big Minh said. He smiled. "Brave, but foolish."

After an hour of bombardment from the Viet Minh's mortars the fire had lifted, and the shrill screams of "*Tien len!*" (Forward!) were heard as the Viet Minh threw themselves across the barbed wire and into the mine-fields, oblivious of their losses. Minh's forces concentrated heavy automatic-weapons fire against the attacking infantry, and one attack after another was

119

smashed as the attackers were cut to pieces. Minh was also able to get support from French artillery batteries now, and they were firing directly into the barbed wire at the charging troops, but still the Viet Minh came. Within an hour it was obvious that the position could no longer be held. The barbed wire entanglements, now covered with a carpet of enemy bodies, had become totally useless as a hindrance. Most of the emplacements for automatic weapons had been blasted to bits by enemy mortars, and the surviving members of Minh's command were rapidly running out of ammunition.

Minh gave the order to fall back to the secondary position, where he had earlier placed two tanks to provide final defensive fire. The tanks, guns depressed to minimum elevation, fired into the screaming human tide. The Viet Minh crawled over the bodies of their comrades and into the teeth of the tanks. The tanks rolled forward, crushing heads, limbs, and chests by the dozens as they moved slowly like chained elephants in the little open space left them. But soon they too were submerged by the seemingly never-ending human wave. Hands clawed at the hatches, trying to pry them open, pushing hand grenades into the gun tubes, firing bursts from their AK-47s into the driving slits, finally destroying them with point-blank satchel charges, which lit up the hulls with the sizzling of white-hot metal. The air was filled with the stench of searing flesh as the crews of both tanks died, roasting alive at their posts.

Big Minh had gone down during the last attack, and Justin waded out through the Viet Minh, slamming them right and left with a rifle butt, and dragged Minh back to the embankment. They rolled down the embankment and into the river, where they remained until the Viet Minh, seemingly satisfied with their victory, withdrew.

There wasn't one man of Big Minh's battalion, a group of over four hundred, left alive, except Big Minh himself, and he was badly wounded. Justin led, dragged, and carried Big Minh back to safety, a feat that required six days to accomplish.

Big Minh and Justin solidified a friendship that had continued from that day.

Big Minh had made arrangements to meet with Justin in a private house in Cholon to discuss the coup. He had instructed Justin to stand on a specific street corner at a specific time, and told him that someone would pick him up and deliver him to the meeting.

At the appointed hour, an old Citroen clattered to the curb, and the driver leaned across the front and opened the door. The driver had a scar that started at his chin, moved up across his mouth, leaving a gap in his lips through which his teeth could be seen, and then went up through his eye socket, where a sightless gray mass of what had been an eye sat in grotesque mockery.

"I am Captain Phat," the driver said. "You will come with me, please?"

Justin got into the car, and they drove away. He tried a couple of times to make conversation, but Captain Phat didn't seem interested. Finally, Justin quit trying and just rode quietly.

The house to which Justin was delivered was not ostentatious, but was quite comfortable by Vietnamese standards. It had an enclosed patio, and Big Minh was sitting on a box beneath a tree, eating a piece of chicken when Justin arrived.

"You will get fat," Justin teased.

"Justin, my friend," Big Minh said, wiping his hand on

his trousers and then extending it, "I am glad you could come. Tell me about your meeting with Tung."

"It was frustrating," Justin said. "I am sure he is acting on Diem's behalf, but I can't prove it. And General McKenzie is committed to Tung. Until Tung shows that he is incapable, or provides us with some other reason for dropping him, McKenzie won't change his position."

"One cannot make a revolution without recruiting an army, and Tung has recruited no one," Big Minh said.

"He wants us to do that for him," Justin replied. "He asked for a list of officers acceptable to the Americans. He says they will form his junta."

"To put a name on such a list is to sign a death warrant," Big Minh said. "What better way to find out who your enemies are than to have a list of them?"

"I agree with you," Justin said.

"You refused?"

"I said I lacked the authority and would have to confer with General McKenzie."

"What will McKenzie say?"

Justin laughed. "He will say nothing, because I won't tell him. I don't trust McKenzie's judgment on this sort of thing. Oh, by the way, I have the timetable. Tung claims that the operation will take place on the tenth of October. He says he will attack Saigon."

If Tung is actually planning an operation, that wouldn't give us much time," Big Minh said. "But I'll start recruiting unit commanders now. Have you decided how you can help?"

"I'll be making preparations, as if to support Tung's operation. The preparations will be the same, and I can merely transfer the support to you when the time comes. But you'll have to keep me informed as to what units you will have in support, who the friendly commanders are, where your headquarters will be, things like that."

Big Minh put his hand on Justin's shoulder. "You are taking a major chance, my friend. I don't know what you call it, but I am sure you must be committing some type of crime against your government."

"At the least, sedition," Justin said grimly. "At the worst, treason. But if it is successful, we'll be able to sweep everything under the rug."

"It will be successful," Minh promised. "And then we will end Diem's oppression."

Big Minh got a faraway look in his eye. "You know that Diem and his brother and his brutal officers and yes-men have driven many good men to the Viet Cong. Most of them are not Communist. They have temporarily allied themselves with the VC in order to seek some justice from our government."

Minh paused, then went on with a smile. "You and I met at the bloody battle of Tu Ba. But there was another who was once close to me and fought at my side in many battles. Today he is the senior VC military commander for this area. He is not really a Communist, but when I send messages to him urging him to rally to us, he thinks it is a trap. He believes the security chiefs in Saigon will wring him dry of intelligence, then push him in front of a firing squad. And as things are today, he is probably right. So, he stays with the Viet Cong. He has no choice. If we had a government that men like him could respect and trust, the VC problem would be solved."

Captain Phat joined them, and they drank a few beers, then Phat offered to take Justin back.

"Phat is ugly now, the result of one of Colonel Doung's little torture chambers," Minh said, running his finger along the scar on Phat's face. "But he is loyal, and he will die for me, as he lost the eye for me. And now, because I have told him to, he will die for you if necessary. Am I not right, Phat?"

"If it is your wish that I be loyal to the American Colonel, then I will be, my General," Phat answered.

"Thank you, Captain Phat," Justin said sincerely. Then with an attempt at a smile, "But I certainly hope your loyalty never has to be proved with your death."

Justin told Big Minh goodbye, and Captain Phat drove him back downtown where he had left the Jeep. Justin returned to the small apartment that he kept.

From the balcony Justin could see the Saigon River. Tonight, he stood at the balcony's edge and watched the black river twinkling as it flowed under the arching lights of the Y Bridge.

After considering what was developing, and wondering what his role would be in it, he went back inside, lay in his bed, and after a few hours of jumbled thoughts, finally fell asleep.

## 16

THE SITUATION IN SAIGON GREW MORE STRAINED; AND concurrent with the intensifying tension was the increasing difference of opinion between the American military in Vietnam and the American Embassy.

This conflict was never more strikingly obvious than during the inspection tour of General Krulak, from the Pentagon, and Joseph Mendenhall of the State Department. The General was to check on the military establishment, meaning MACV, and the Foreign Service officer was to roam the countryside.

MACV, which had the responsibility for General Krulak's inspection, arranged his tour. They provided statistical data, charts, captured weapons, repatriated VC, and pacified villages; it wasn't an insight into the country, but an illusion of knowledge, created by the image-makers of MACV. General Krulak saw the packaging, but he didn't see the product, and he came away believing the progress report MACV presented. "The situation is good," he said. "And the people are rallying to Diem's support."

But Mendenhall, whose inspection was being orchestrated by the embassy people in Vietnam, was shown just those things that would strengthen the U.S. commitment to remove Diem. "The situation is very bad," Mendenhall said when he returned. "The people are becoming more disenchanted with Diem with the passing of every day."

Newspapers reported that President Kennedy had listened to the sharply contrasting reports and then asked, "Were you two gentlemen in the same country?"

Shortly after the inspection tour, Colonel Rogers sat in his office listening to the report of an American intelligence agent, Lucien Conein. General McKenzie had telephoned Rogers and told him to meet with the man who apparently had some information that was vital to Operation Valkyrie. "Colonel," Conein said quietly, "Diem is engaged in some intensive maneuvering that may well change the entire complexion of the Vietnam situation. He is negotiating in secret with the Viet Cong. He has had several meetings with a man whom we call 'Uncle.' Uncle is one of the most senior members of the VC political arm."

Colonel Rogers very fastidiously inserted a cigarette into a holder and lit it before he answered. He held the cigarette away from him so that he could avoid the curling smoke as much as possible. "What is the purpose of the meetings?" he asked.

"To conclude some sort of peace arrangement, I suppose," Conein said. "I believe Diem is offering a coalition government in order to get a cease-fire. That way he would be free to deal with the enemies of his government. Meaning, right now, the coup elements."

"How many times has he met with them?" Rogers asked.

"Three or four times. They are having difficulty

reaching an agreement, but they must be making some progress, because the meetings are still going on."

Rogers got up from his desk and walked over to the window. An old woman shuffled along outside carrying a long pole with a large burlap bag attached to each end. Two young boys scurried around gathering tin cans to put into the bags. A third child, just a baby, gurgled contentedly from its perch in a pocket formed by a blanket wrapped around the old woman's back.

"Who is the man Diem is meeting? This 'Uncle'—do you have any more on him?" Rogers asked.

"He's their top theorist. He developed their people-to-people campaign—and believe me, it's effective," the agent answered. "With little effort, he manages to credit the Viet Cong with everything good and blame the United States for everything bad."

"Do you know his name?"

"It is Cao Ba Nguyen," Conein answered. Colonel Rogers returned to his desk and looked over at the American agent, who had not moved from his chair during the entire visit.

"What exactly do you want from me?" Colonel Rogers asked, clamping the cigarette holder tightly in his teeth.

"Nothing, Colonel," Conein answered easily. "I have the obligation to bring it to your attention, but the decision as to what to do about it will depend entirely on you." Conein pulled a bent cigarette from a crumpled package and stuck it in his mouth. His face remained expressionless.

"I see," Rogers said. He removed a tissue from a box and pinched the cigarette out of his holder, then dropped it neatly into an ashtray and closed the lid over the top. Rogers brushed his hands together, then smiled hesitantly at the agent. "Well, thank you very much for the information...uh...I'm sorry, I don't think I got your name."

"We won't worry about that, Colonel," the agent replied, standing quickly and extending his hand. "I must be going now. I hope the information was of some use to you."

Conein left without telling Rogers his name.

Rogers returned to his desk after the American left and thought about the best way to deal with the situation. It was delicate and couldn't be mishandled, but to let it go without any action whatever would be disastrous. And it was up to him. It was obvious that General McKenzie meant him to handle it or he would never have sent the mysterious agent to see him.

Rogers opened the middle drawer of his desk and removed a small blue box with a clear plastic top. The label on the box said MEYER'S SILVER PLATE INSIGNIA, and inside, pinned to a red card, was the star of a Brigadier General. Colonel Rogers wanted to pin that star on his collar more than anything else in the world. It was the driving ambition of his life. He knew that the number of officers who made it to General's rank was abysmally small, and that only those who managed to attract attention to themselves, favorably, would ever succeed. He was perhaps in such a position right now by engineering Valkyrie. And as the responsible officer it was his obligation not to let anything happen which would impede the thrust of events toward the coup. Rogers would have to have Cao Ba Nguyen killed.

Rogers took another cigarette from his silver case, placed it in his holder, and thought about what he would have to do. It was an extremely unpleasant business, and that bothered him. He tried to tell himself that it shouldn't bother him, that he was a professional soldier and had worked on plans involving the death of many. So why should the thought of one man's death—and that man an enemy to his country—bother him?

Rogers lit his cigarette with a silver desk lighter, and then wiped the lighter with a tissue and put it back in its place. He considered his discomfort, and believed that he had the answer. It was the euphemistic value of depersonalization. It is hard to get emotionally involved with the abstract notion of the deaths of a depersonalized "many." Millions of Jews were killed during World War II, but the real, immediate impact can be felt only when one considers the tragedy of a single human being, and not of humanity. The death of Anne Frank can bring a person to tears. The death of "millions of Jews" can bring on horror, disgust, a sense of shared guilt, but rarely tears.

But it had to be done, so Rogers put the troublesome thoughts out of his mind. He replaced those thoughts with the mental images of what he would look like with stars pinned to his collar, and what it would be like when he was a general.

General Vernon E. Rogers.

It would be glorious.

## 17

ON THE NIGHT OF THE TWENTY-THIRD OF SEPTEMBER, A gala ball was held in the villa of the West German Embassy. It was well attended, and beautiful women in colorful dresses and flashing jewels, and handsome young men in medal-bedecked uniforms or elegant cutaways moved through the tiled halls. For a brief instant in the broiling intrigue of plot and counterplot, Saigon seemed to recover some of its lost elegance and give credibility to its onetime reputation as the Paris of the Orient.

The Americans were represented in full force at the party, and there were many from the embassy and MACV in attendance. There were, however, dissensions beneath the surface facade of glamour. Fissures had developed between the embassy and the military, and even between individuals within the same sections. The Krulak-Mendenhall trip had accomplished nothing. The investigators had come up with such diametrically opposed points of view that neither party was able to make any headway. So, word had come from Washington that Secretary MacNamara and General Taylor would be arriving in Saigon on the twenty-fourth of September to look into the matter personally.

Justin was at the party, and so was Le.

"Good evening, Madam Doung," Justin said. "May I pour you a glass of punch?"

"Yes," Le replied. "That would be nice. Thank you." Le handed her cup to Justin just as Colonel Rogers approached, and Le, with a shy smile and a pleasant greeting for Rogers, left.

"Colonel Barclay," Rogers said, pouring himself a cup of punch and being very careful of his dress whites, "Secretary MacNamara and General Taylor arrive tomorrow. Will you be meeting them?"

"I'll be at the airport," Justin replied. "I'm not scheduled to brief them at any time, so I doubt if I will actually meet either of them."

"I need to see you after the ceremony at the airport," Rogers said. "I want you to arrange a meeting for me with a local national."

"Who do you want to meet?" Justin asked, his curiosity aroused.

"Someone who is outside the official scheme. That's why I feel you can best manage it for me. How is everything with General Tung, by the way? Is everything going all right?"

"Colonel Rogers, Tung is without doubt the worst possible choice for us," Justin replied. "He couldn't possibly have any support. Suppose we draw up a list of officers acceptable to us and suggest a junta committee to Tung?"

"No," Rogers said flatly. "We will continue to let Tung handle everything. He can select his own junta."

Justin smiled. It was exactly the answer he wanted.

Now he could refuse to provide Tung with the list, and he could do so with Colonel Rogers' official backing.

"Colonel, why not drop Tung and throw our support to someone like Big Minh? He enjoys popular support," Justin said.

"That's exactly why we don't want him," Rogers answered. "Popular generals will find it easy to continue a military government indefinitely. Unpopular generals will themselves be thrown out, and then others, civilians, our civilians, can be brought in. And the person I wish to contact tomorrow is just such a civilian."

"What is his name?"

"I'll tell you tomorrow, just after the reception at the airport," Rogers said.

At the airport the next day the temporary truce that seemed to have been in effect for the party the evening before fell away. Dissension between the military and embassy people seemed to hang in the air like a heavy charge of electricity. It was especially visible between Lodge and Harkins, who stood in icy silence, waiting for the plane. It extended to their staffs, and men who had worked together and liked each other during the Nolting-Harkins era, barely spoke to each other under the Lodge-Harkins administration.

The extent of the dissension was embarrassingly apparent when Secretary MacNamara deplaned. Two members of the embassy staff purposely blocked off General Harkins so that the ambassador would be the first to greet the Secretary. The move caused General Harkins to shout out in anger, "Gentlemen, please, allow me through to greet the Secretary!"

Justin knew that the visit would accomplish nothing. Neither MacNamara nor Taylor stood the slightest chance of finding the truth no matter how good their intentions might be. Justin shook his head slowly, then turned away from the scene in disgust. "Colonel Barclay?"

Justin turned to see Colonel Rogers standing there. "Ah, yes, you wanted me to arrange a meeting for you," Justin said. "Are you prepared to tell me with whom the meeting is to be?"

"Yes. Do you have a Jeep? I want to drive around while we talk. I don't wish to be overheard."

"Oh? More intrigue?" Justin asked.

"Why not? This is the mysterious Orient, isn't it?" Rogers replied with a smile. "Hey, how about us going somewhere for a good cold beer? We could relax while we talk."

Justin looked at Colonel Rogers in surprise. Rogers seemed to be making a genuine effort to be friendly.

"Would you mind going to a bami-bam stand?" Justin asked. "We could keep an eye on the Jeep, and we wouldn't be bothered by anyone. And the beer is cold and cheap."

"That sounds fine," Rogers said. They reached the Jeep, and Rogers slid into the seat and began carefully placing a cigarette in his holder.

"Any problems?" Justin asked as he unlocked the chain that passed through the steering wheel.

"No," Rogers answered easily. "As I said, I just want to meet someone, and I think you can best arrange it."

A small boy ran up to the Jeep and held out his hand, claiming to have guarded the Jeep for Justin. Justin smiled at him, spoke a few words in Vietnamese, and gave him a few pastries.

"You...you really do like these people, don t you?" Rogers asked, his tone almost one of surprise, as if for the first time he believed that Justin might really be sincere.

"Yes," Justin answered as he drove away.

"Why?"

"I don't know. Maybe it's because they have an innocence, some sort of purity of character that I find appealing."

"Innocence? Purity of character? Why, they'll steal us blind—and they are absolutely impossible to comprehend."

"Their emotions run deep," Justin said. "Mine do too, so perhaps I relate. Who do you want me to locate for you?"

"A man named Cao Ba Nguyen."

"Nguyen? I know him," Justin said. "That is, if the one I know is the same man."

"What is Nguyen like?" Rogers Asked.

"An older man, respected, very smart. He spent almost thirty years in Paris, and returned to Vietnam just before the war, when everyone else was going the other way. Is it the same guy you know?"

"It could be," Justin said. "The Nguyen I know is an old man, and he mentioned having been in Paris. He's an excellent chess player."

"Chess?" Rogers said. "I'm afraid that's no help to me. Would you recognize his picture?"

"I think so," Justin replied.

They pulled alongside the curb near one of the beer stands, and Justin motioned to the vendor for two beers. "God, that's good!" Rogers said, taking a long drink, and then wiping his mouth with a handkerchief. He pulled a picture from his shirt pocket.

"It isn't a very good picture," he apologized. "It was

taken with a telephoto, I understand. But it is a recent picture."

Justin looked at the picture and smiled. "Yes, it's the same man," he said. "I can take you to see him right now, if you'd like."

"No," Rogers said. "I'd better not go to him. See if you can arrange a meeting for me."

"Nguyen will meet you only if he wants to," Justin said. "I won't try and force him."

"I'm sure you won't," Rogers said.

"I'll go see him now," Justin offered.

Rogers finished his beer, then wiped his mouth and his hands fastidiously, and put his folded handkerchief away neatly in his pocket before he spoke again.

"Colonel Barclay, if you don't mind, I'd like to wait at your apartment. If you can arrange a meeting, you can inform me there."

"Sure," Justin said, a little confused. "My apartment isn't all that comfortable, but you are welcome to use it."

"It's just that I wish to remain discreet in this matter," Rogers explained.

"You're welcome to it, Colonel," Justin said again.

Justin dropped Colonel Rogers off at his apartment and then drove to Phu Coung to try to find Cao Ba Nguyen. He parked near the river then returned to the same sidewalk cafe where he had first encountered Nguyen. The vendor smiled as he recognized Justin and asked him if he wanted a fish.

"Thank you, no," Justin replied. "But I would take some of your fine tea."

The old man nodded happily and poured tea from a steaming kettle into a beautiful and delicate porcelain cup.

"Old one, do you remember the wise man with whom I played *co tuong*?" Justin asked.

A quick shadow flitted across the old man's eyes, and he put the tea kettle down before he answered haltingly. "I remember you played a game. I do not know with whom the game was played."

"Surely you remember," Justin said. "Cao Ba Nguyen, the elder?"

"I do not know such a person," the old man said, averting his eyes from Justin's gaze.

Justin realized then that for some reason the old man wouldn't tell him. He didn't press the matter, but merely finished his tea and made some pleasantries about the sun on the river. After he had finished his tea, he walked through the marketplace and then through the village. Everyone who saw him recognized him as the American *co tuong* player. But no one would admit to even knowing Cao Ba Nguyen. Finally, frustrated in his efforts, Justin decided to return to Saigon.

"What's the whole story on Nguyen?" Justin asked Rogers after he returned.

"There is no whole story," Rogers replied. "I told you —I think he would be good in a post-Diem government. I want to talk with him about it."

"I agree with you," Justin said. "I met him, and I like him. But now I can't find him, and for some reason the people seem to be hiding him from me. I can't understand why. He wasn't hiding before. He was in full view for several hours. We played a game together."

"That was different. You weren't looking for him then. Now you are, and they are suspicious."

"Suspicious? Suspicious of what? Colonel Rogers, is Nguyen a member of the National Liberation Front?"

"Yes," Rogers said.

"Well, that explains it. You should have told me before I went. Had I known, I would have been prepared and could still have reached him. Now I'm afraid that I may have missed the— No, wait. I still think I might be able to reach him."

"How?"

"Le—Madam Doung. She seemed to know him quite well. Perhaps she can locate him for me."

"Good," Rogers said. "Try it, then. It's very important that I see him."

"Wait here," Justin said, leaving the apartment again.

"WHY DO YOU WANT HIM?" Le asked when Justin told her that he wanted to contact Nguyen.

"Le, I can't tell you. I will tell you that it is important."

"Doung will not know of this?" Le asked. "Nguyen is wanted by the Diem Government. Doung has said he will kill Nguyen on sight."

"Doung has nothing to do with this," Justin said. "This is an American affair."

"It is very dangerous for Nguyen."

"But I saw him the other day. I played *co tuong* with him, and we spoke of chess and other things. He didn't appear to be frightened."

"He was with his people. No one who wished him harm could have approached him."

"Le, Nguyen is VC, isn't he?"

"Yes," Le replied.

"If he is, you'll never get to him. Especially since you're the wife of Colonel Doung, head of the Special Police."

"Yes, I am Colonel Doung's wife," Le said. "But I am also Cao Ba Nguyen's daughter."

Le went into her bedroom, leaving Justin gaping in open-mouthed shock. She changed from the chic dress she was wearing into the black loose-fitting pajama-type shirt and trousers, and she put a conical straw hat on her head. She exchanged her fashionable shoes for woven sandals, then she had Justin drive her to the bus stop.

"I will come to your apartment to tell you where the meeting will be," Le said as she moved away from the Jeep and was swallowed up by the mass of humanity waiting to catch the bus.

True to her word, Le returned that night bearing the address where Nguyen would be waiting. Rogers thanked her and started for the door.

"Don't you want me to come with you?" Justin asked.

"No," Rogers said. "Uh...I think it would be better if I saw him alone."

After Rogers had left, Justin turned to Le. "Is the fact that your father is a VC the reason you were embarrassed to meet him the other day?" he asked.

"Not entirely," Le said. "And I wasn't embarrassed. Perhaps a little frightened. Doung wants very much to kill him."

"Even though he is your father?"

"I think especially because he is my father," Le replied.

"I can see why you were frightened," Justin said

"Perhaps the war will end shortly."

"What makes you think that?"

"My father. He speaks for the National Liberation Front. He has been meeting with Diem, and now he meets with an American. He was very excited over it." Justin sat up.

"He's been meeting with Diem? How do you know?"

138

"He told me tonight," Le said. "He said agreement with Diem was very near." Justin laughed.

"What is it?" Le asked.

"Oh, nothing really. I was just thinking that if your father is right, Diem has jerked the rug out from under a lot of people. There are going to be several red faces. Why, I'll bet they'd—" Justin was going to say, "stop it if they could," but he didn't say it. Because it had been meant lightheartedly. Now he suddenly realized that it was probably deadly serious. Rogers did intend to stop the meetings and prevent any agreement. Justin's face blanched.

"Le, where was your father to meet Rogers?" he asked.

"Beneath Y Bridge," Le answered. "Why?"

"Perhaps nothing," Justin said. "But I think I'd better find your father."

"Justin, I don't understand. And you are frightening me," Le said.

"Le, I can't say anymore. But your father may be in trouble. I've got to get to him as quickly as I can."

"I'm going with you," Le said.

Justin drove through the evening traffic, running through lights and paying no attention to the police whistles that shrilled angrily as he raced by.

Justin knew that it was foolish to drive this way. It took approximately twenty minutes to get from Justin's apartment to the Y Bridge, and Rogers had been gone for nearly an hour. This meant Rogers had been there a long time already. Justin couldn't turn back the clock, but he could vent his frustration on the wheel, so he drove with reckless abandon.

Just before Y Bridge the driver of an old French truck, which was so loaded with baskets that even the cab of the truck was covered with them, pulled onto the road without looking. Justin had no time to stop and had barely got his foot onto the brake pedal when the Jeep slammed into the truck with a crash. The impact caused Justin's hand to snap off the steering wheel at the column, and then, still holding the wheel, smash his fist through the windshield. He wound up half lying across the hood.

Le, amazingly, had seen the accident approaching and had braced herself so that she wasn't injured at all. People began crowding around the Jeep. The accident appeared to be much worse than it really was. The Jeep was smashed in the front and glass was scattered everywhere. But Justin was the only one whose injury would have been looked at by a doctor. If there had been one. And if he had waited. But he jumped out and started for the bridge, now less than a block away.

"Justin, are you all right?" Le asked anxiously.

"Come on," Justin said, walking quickly. "I'm not hurt. We've got to get there."

They scrambled down the concrete embankment, and then along the riverbank to the underpass of the bridge. Justin saw it then. He almost missed it, because the water was so black and it was in the shadows, but there was no mistaking what it was. It was a man's body, floating face down, bumping gently against the pilings as the water lapped quietly to the bank.

Justin took Le and tried to turn her around so she couldn't see, but Le sensed something and pulled away from him. Then she saw her father's body. "Murderers!" She screamed. "You did this!"

"Le," Justin called out in anguish, "I didn't know—" Le started running down the bank of the river, melting into the crowd of people who had come from the scene of the wreck to the new point of excitement. Justin tried to follow her, but he lost her.

A burning rage gripped him, and he thought of Colonel Rogers and what Rogers had done. He caught a cyclo and rode to MACV headquarters, but Rogers wasn't there, so he went to see McKenzie at his villa.

Rogers was with McKenzie, sitting in a chair across the desk from him. Justin slammed the door shut and crossed the room in a rush.

"You murdering son-of-a-bitch!" he yelled.

"What? What's wrong with you?" Rogers asked, standing up, seemingly surprised at Justin's behavior.

Justin threw a roundhouse right at Rogers, catching him on the temple and knocking him across General McKenzie's desk. Papers, pens, books, and all the rest of the paraphernalia on top of McKenzie's desk went flying as Rogers slid the length of it and then fell off on the other side. Justin grabbed him by the collar and lifted him up, then knocked him down again.

"Colonel Barclay, I order you to be at ease!" McKenzie shouted. "Be at ease, sir!"

Rogers didn't punch back. Instead, he covered his face with his arms and bent double. He was shouting to General McKenzie to pull Justin off him.

Justin didn't hit him again. Instead, he just shoved Rogers away from him with disgust.

"What is the meaning of this?" General McKenzie asked, livid with rage.

"Rogers had me set up a meeting for him so he could murder a man," Justin said. "Cold-blooded murder."

"I didn't do it," Rogers said. He was dabbing at his cut lip with his handkerchief. "That's why I'm here now," he said. "Nguyen was dead when I got there."

"You mean you deny you killed him?" Justin asked,

his voice rising in pitch to register his anger and disbelief.

"That's exactly what I mean," Rogers said.

"Colonel Rogers came to me this evening to report that the man with whom he was to meet was dead," McKenzie said. "Is that what you are concerned about?"

"Who could have done it if Rogers didn't do it?" Justin asked.

"I have no idea," General McKenzie replied. "He was, after all, a wanted man. I suppose it isn't out of the question that he was killed by the police."

"I didn't do it," Rogers said again.

"You are lying," Justin said, looking at Rogers. "You killed him because you found out he was meeting with Diem. You were trying to protect your coup plans."

"You can substantiate that charge, I suppose?" General McKenzie asked icily.

"I don't have to substantiate it. I know it's true," Justin said.

"In the absence of more conclusive evidence, I've no choice but to accept Colonel Rogers' version of the incident," General McKenzie said. "I'd advise you to apologize to Colonel Rogers or stand ready to face charges of assault against a senior officer."

"I've no intention of apologizing to that murdering bastard," Justin said. "And you've no intention of bringing me before a court-martial. You couldn't afford it if the truth were known."

"We'll just see about that," Colonel Rogers spat, finally regaining some of his composure. "General McKenzie, I wish to prefer charges against Lieutenant Colonel Justin Barclay."

"Don't be an ass, Vern," McKenzie said calmly. "He's right. We can't afford to court-martial him."

18

THE CRASHING GLASS CAUSED EVERYONE IN THE BAR TO duck from the flying splinters. A few jagged pieces of the mirror hung in the frame, and their dagger-like slivers reflected the face of Justin Barclay, twisted in rage.

A bar girl, her eyes cobra-lidded and darkly painted, moved over to Barclay.

"Maybe if you'll buy me Saigon Tea, you'll feel better," the girl suggested.

"That bastard Rogers did it, I know he did. I should have killed the son-of-a-bitch."

"You buy me Saigon tea?" the girl asked again.

"Yes, but go somewhere else to drink it. I'm in no mood for company.

THE PILOT ADJUSTED HIS CONTROLS, and the helicopter began its descent into My Tho.

"This is where you get off, Colonel Barclay."

"Thank you," Justin said.

The contrast between the elegant villa where Le lived in Saigon, and the home of her sister in My Tho was unbelievable. Her sister's house was built on the river's edge, and the back part of it was on stilts, actually protruding out over the water. The house was covered with sheet tin made from pressed soft drink and beer cans. A naked child sat in the dirt, and others ran alongside Justin, laughing and shouting with excitement.

An old man was sitting on the porch of the house holding a fishing pole. He looked at Justin but didn't speak.

"Are you catching much fish?" Justin asked.

"No," the old man answered. "I have told the fish I do not want trouble with them. I only appear to fish, so that I may sit here and sleep, and the young ones will not say that I am lazy. You are American, the one they call Justin?"

"Yes," Justin answered. You know me?"

"I am the father of the husband of Le's sister," the old man said. "Le has spoken of you."

"Where is she? I'd like to see her," Justin replied, almost desperately, but with respect and courtesy.

"I think now is not a good time," the old man said.

"Why not?" Justin replied. "I've got to see her— it's very important. I wish I could make you understand."

"I understand," the old man said. "Now would not be a good time."

"When would be a good time?" Justin asked.

"Maybe there is no good time," the old man answered

"But I must see her," Justin said. "I must talk with her and tell her that—" Justin stopped in mid-sentence. Tell her what? he thought. That the death of her father wasn't his fault? But it was. And he was right now engaged in the effort to bring about a coup that would in all probability cost the life of her husband. Even if he thought she could understand all that, he still wouldn't be able to tell her. "Never mind," Justin finally said, quietly.

Justin turned to leave, and then, with a start, saw Le was behind him, standing quietly.

"Why did you come?" Le asked. She was dressed in peasant garb. Her hair was combed smoothly, and she had no makeup on her face. There was absolutely no resemblance between the woman who stood there and the glamorous creature whose face had graced the pages of magazines and newspapers around the world.

"I had to see you."

"You killed my father," Le said.

"Le, you know I didn't."

"You asked me to get him. Your friend killed him—and you could have prevented it. "

"Be reasonable," Justin pleaded. "You know I had no idea of what was going to happen. If I had, of course I would have prevented it."

"If you had no idea, why did you suddenly rush to him?" Le asked.

"Because I happened to realize that—Le, there are circumstances here that I can't disclose. Believe me, I didn't want your father killed. If I had known they were going to do it, I would have attempted to stop it. You must believe that I didn't want him killed."

"Perhaps you didn't want it," Le conceded. "But you are riding the tiger. What else will the tiger have you do? Perhaps even kill me? I will not ride the tiger with you."

Justin started to speak again, but Le turned and ran to the house, her sandals making a soft whisper on the path. Justin didn't run after her. Instead,

he returned to the heliport just in time to catch a

145

flight back to Saigon. He was fortunate, because he had no fellow passengers to intrude into his thoughts. Only the door gunners rode in back with him, and they sat in silence behind their M-60 machine guns and watched the changing pattern of the Vietnam landscape unfold beneath them. Occasionally one of them would speak into his lip mike to another member of the crew, but Justin, who wasn't wearing a helmet or a headset, was excluded from the conversation. And he was glad.

ELECTIONS to the National Assembly took place on September 27. Justin, as an advisor to the Special Police, was also selected as an observer to the official proceedings. He was to tour several polling places within his area and then report on the elections to an American advisory committee.

Justin had never seen such a burlesque. He sat in one of the polling houses and watched the voters come through. First the voter would step hesitantly, fearfully, through the door. Inside, there were armed policemen and soldiers. A table was set up, and a clerk sat behind it.

"Come, come," the chief of the poll guards would call. "We don't have all day. Do you have a registration card?"

The voter would produce his card, and it would be stamped, indicating that he had voted. For the average voter, the stamping of the card was the only important part of the entire procedure. Because anyone who was searched and found without a voting stamp on his card after election day could find himself in big trouble.

The next step was to pick up the ballots. Each political party had its own ballot, so that although the election was supposedly secret, the only privacy the voter had was when he actually dropped the ballots into the box. Everyone knew how he voted, because they knew which ballots he picked up.

The voters approached the ballots with great caution and fear. If they picked up the wrong ones, then they could be in trouble. It was all very confusing, since there were nearly 600 names to consider, and almost 60 ballots, each with its own symbol. The voters were therefore appreciative when the local policemen provided them with assistance by selecting the ballots for them.

However, not all the voters were frightened and hesitant. There were several truckloads of soldiers who toured from poll to poll and voted at each of them. They became quite proficient at it, and proudly displayed their expertise to the local voters at each new polling place. Since the same soldiers ran across Justin at several different polls, they began speaking to him and making jokes with him each time they encountered him. They made no attempt to hide the fact that they were voting several times. In fact, many of them didn't even consider that what they were doing was wrong. They were acting on orders from their officers, and that was that.

Justin realized that the election was an exercise in futility anyway, because the upcoming coup would negate the results. So, he refused to allow himself the luxury of getting too upset over the travesty. Nonetheless he found it difficult to believe that MACV not only accepted the claimed results of the election but praised it as evidence of the success of the democratic process.

MACV parroted the official election results, which were that 6,329,831 out of 6,809,078 qualified voters had voted. Among the successful candidates for office were Ngo Dinh Nhu and his wife, Madam Nhu, who, according to officially released figures, received 99.9 and 99.8 percent of the votes in their respective constituencies.

This was heralded as a great democratic triumph.

## 19

THE PEOPLE OF THE VILLAGE OF PHONG BAC HAD TURNED out to honor President Diem by holding an elephant race. A reviewing stand stood in the center of the village square, and the yellow and red Vietnamese flags fluttered everywhere.

There seemed to be a genuine spirit of enthusiasm among the people, although it may have been over the excitement of the race itself rather than the presence of the President. Women and children were laughing, and the men were busily engaged in placing their bets before the race began.

Diem sat on the reviewing stand along with a few other dignitaries. The elephants that were to race were being paraded by, and the attention of most of the people was held by that spectacle. But Diem and Father DePaul, a Jesuit priest and a longtime friend, talked.

You are absolutely certain the Americans killed Nguyen?" Father DePaul asked.

"There's no doubt about it," Diem said. He took a bite

of fresh pineapple and smiled at one of the villagers who waved at him.

"But why?" Father DePaul asked. "It would seem to me that the Americans would be pleased with any action toward a rapprochement. Surely that is so, is it not?"

A great cheer went up then, and a white baby elephant, an extreme rarity and the symbol of good luck in Vietnam, was led to the stand. The elephant's trainer got the elephant to stand on its front two legs, and the village chief made the announcement that the elephant was being given as a gift to Diem.

"Thank you," Diem answered. "And I would like to arrange to keep him here, among happy people. I will come to see him often."

The villagers applauded again.

"It's the way I handle all my animals," Diem said with a smile to Father DePaul. "I have tigers, elephants, monkeys, and snakes at villages all over Vietnam. Perhaps after the coup I can go into another line of work. I can open a zoo."

"Ah," said Father DePaul, who was still thinking of the killing of Cao Ba Nguyen. "I know the reason the Americans killed Nguyen. They knew that he was VC, but did not know you were meeting with him."

Diem gave a small, almost resigned, laugh. "I wish that was so," he said. "But I'm afraid he was killed because the Americans did know I was meeting with him."

"But if they knew, there would be no reason for killing him. Why did they?" Father DePaul asked.

"The Communist threat seems to have moved down in the order of American priorities," Diem said. "Number One now, and most important to the American ambassador, is the determination to eliminate my government."

"Coups and rumors of coups," Father DePaul said. "It is a fact of life that you must live with. But these coup attempts have occurred before, and you survived. You will survive this one as well."

"This is the first time there has ever been a plot organized against me from outside my country," Diem said. "And by the Americans. Father DePaul, I have been very foolish. I have allowed myself to become so dependent on American aid that I cannot survive without its vigorous support. And now, for the United States to turn against me...it's my death knell."

Diem made a fist, squeezing it so tightly that his knuckles turned white. "Trapped. Trapped. I am trapped."

The elephants were moved to the starting line, and the crashing of a gong signaled the beginning of the race. The ground nearly shook as the large beasts began running through the village.

Father DePaul," Diem said, "you enjoy a good relationship with the Americans here. Go see Cabot Lodge. Tell him that there is no problem that we cannot work out. Make him realize that my government is stable, and that the turmoil and confusion of a change now would cause great harm. Tell him that I make this plea for the welfare of my country and not out of concern for my own life."

"Surely you can't believe your life is in danger?" Father DePaul asked. "If, as you say, the Americans are primarily behind the coup, then they would guarantee your safety."

Diem smiled and put his hand on the shoulder of his

friend. "It is so marvelous that no one believes the Americans capable of evil deeds. I think it is the product of their Madison Avenue. They can sell their own image as easily as they sell underarm deodorant."

Father DePaul looked Diem in the eyes. "You—you really are afraid for your life, aren't you?"

"No," Diem said calmly. "Not fearful, resigned. We all must die—it is just a matter of when. There is an old Vietnamese saying that goes, 'The morning bloom that lives for but an hour differs not at heart from the mighty tree whose life covers a thousand years'"

Another roar from the crowd signaled the end of the race. The victorious elephant and rider came back through the village street toward the reviewing stand.

"Mister President, will you award the winner?" the village chief asked.

Diem took a lei of flowers. He held them for a moment, then looked around the village at the people who had crowded forward to watch the ceremony. "Mr. Vo, when was the last time any of my generals was here?'

"Your generals, Excellency?" Vo asked, his face plainly showing confusion. What generals are you speaking of?

"General Minh, General Kahn, General Don, General Dinh. When did they last visit your village?"

"I do not know these men you speak of," Vo said. He bowed his head in shame. "I am sorry if I have offended you by not knowing your friends."

Diem spoke in French to Father DePaul. "You see. My generals do not have the support of the people, Father. They don't even know the people." He waved his arm grandly, taking in the crowd. "My people," he said.

Diem let his arm drop and stood silent for a brief instant. "And yet, despite the fact that the people belong to me, the army belongs to the Americans. And they will use it to get rid of me."

Diem smiled again and walked across the stand to place the lei around the neck of the winner.

"Diem, leave now. Absent yourself from the country. Don't stay here to be murdered," Father DePaul pleaded.

"And become a laughable creature like Emperor Bao Dai?" Diem asked with a smirk. "To issue statements from exile on the Riviera, which no one reads? I cannot do that. There is much to be done here, and my country needs me. I cannot abandon them to the foolish games of the Americans and my ambitious generals. Besides, I am safe for a while longer. I don't think even the Americans will attempt a coup during an international conference— and there are many Asian and international conferences to be conducted for the remainder of this year. I think the coup will come in January."

The village elders escorted Diem to a large clearing where all the women of the village had laid out food that they had prepared. Several pleaded with him to "buy this, Mr. President," and Diem attempted to oblige them all. They were obviously flattered by his presence, and Diem was obviously happy with his reception. He appeared to have all the earmarks of a popular leader—a "man of the people."

Father DePaul watched the proceedings and clucked his tongue in quiet contemplation. Diem had many faults, as did all men of power. But Diem was more than a mere man, or even a President. Diem was a symbol— the first visible sign of independence for the Vietnamese in over two thousand years. If the Americans removed Diem and replaced his government with another, even though it might be a Vietnamese government, the people of Vietnam would lose their sense of independence, perhaps forever.

Father DePaul hoped that the United Sates would not be foolish enough to make such a mistake.

HAD IT NOT BEEN FOR THE FACT THAT IT WAS THE RAINY season, Saigon might well have come apart on its own during early October even without the aid of coup plotters. The Buddhists kept up their protests, and on the fifth day of October, another Buddhist monk committed suicide by fire. Nhu, in the name of his brother, continued the government harassment of them.

The college students who had begun their protests in sympathy with the Buddhists in September had spread the fervor of their demonstrations from the universities down through the high schools and into the elementary schools. Nhu reacted with force, occupying the schools with his police and special forces. Estimates of from 20 to 500 Buddhists and students were killed, and over 3,000 were put into jail.

The revolutionary fever gripped everyone then. Merchants, taxi drivers, dock workers, bar girls, and even Civil Service workers began to coalesce into a united front against the government. There were talks of widespread strikes to cripple the economy and force the government to come to terms. However, the people realized that the black market and extralegal activities were so entrenched that the economy could not be effectively disrupted, so no organized strikes occurred.

There were several individual acts against the government, but without organization they had no impact. Added to the lack of organization were the daily rains, which interrupted all activity, stopping individual incidents here and there before they could link together and grow of their own accord. The flags and banners of revolution and government alike hung heavy and sodden in the rains.

But the rain didn't defuse the simmering rebellion. It just put a temporary lid on it. The insurrection continued to boil, and the steaming heat of the city formed a great pressure cooker, building up more and more toward a great explosion.

ANTOINE MOUCHETTE WAS SITTING on his veranda watching the rain and contemplating the current situation. Mouchette was a survivor. He had survived the first restive stirrings of independence before World War II, and he had survived the Japanese occupation. After the war, he had cooperated with Ho Chi Minh when Ho Chi Minh had proclaimed an independent Vietnam with a declaration of independence, which read in part: "All men are created equal. They are endowed by their creator with certain inalienable rights; among these are life, liberty and the pursuit of happiness."

Mouchette had to cooperate with Ho Chi Minh for only ten days, because ten days after the Vietnamese declaration of independence the British, in accordance with an arrangement made at Potsdam, arrived in Saigon to administer the territory south of the 16th Parallel, while the Nationalist Chinese arrived in Hanoi to administer the North. Mouchette cooperated with the British in the South, and when he had dealings in the North he cooperated with the Chinese. He survived quite admirably. In early 1946 Mouchette welcomed the return of his countrymen and once more cooperated with the French. But with the return of the French the old longing for independence sprang up again, and the Viet Minh began a revolutionary war. Mouchette cooperated with them when he had to, and with the French when he had to. Finally, a partial settlement eliminated the French entirely, and Mouchette found that if he was to continue to survive, he would have to extend his cooperation to several elements.

There was the government of Emperor Bao Dai, the official, though absent, ruler of South Vietnam. There was also a very strong gang of bandits and river pirates who had formed a quasi-political party known as the Binh Xuyen. The Binh Xuyen, through mutual cooperation with Emperor Bao Dai, controlled the Saigon city police, the national security police, and all gaming houses, opium dens, and brothels.

Mouchette convinced both Bao Dai and General Le Van Vien, commander of the Binh Xuyen, that he was loyal, and he got through that period quite profitably. In late 1955 Ngo Dinh Diem, who was Bao Dai's appointed Premier, launched an offensive against the Binh Xuyen, defeating them and breaking their power forever. Bao Dai, who was himself in Paris, promptly dismissed Diem from office. Diem retaliated by declaring South Vietnam a republic and himself president.

And Mouchette began to cooperate with Diem and

his brothers—especially Nhu—since they were now his key to survival.

But Diem's government had not been unopposed, and the remaining elements of the Viet Minh reorganized into the National Liberation Front, or Viet Cong. The VC started a new war, and Mouchette found that his survival sometimes depended on his cooperation with them.

Now the Americans had intervened, and Antoine Mouchette's villa had become the social hallmark of gracious living. Senior American civilians and military deemed his friendship an honor and were frequently his guests.

Mouchette's survival was not threatened by the fact that he cooperated with everyone. His favors were not something to be jealously hoarded. In fact, everyone let him survive because he was what he was, a haven in the midst of turmoil. No one could afford to take the action that would eliminate the only truly neutral element. Mouchette survived for the same reason that the warring countries of Europe had let Switzerland survive. A known neutral is better than a questionable partisan.

Mouchette couldn't exactly be classified as a neutral, because he was free with his support when it served his interests. Right now, for example, he had promised General Tung his support, and had fulfilled that promise so far. He had exercised influence over General McKenzie to solidify McKenzie's backing of Tung. He had also passed information back to Tung, which he had received from McKenzie. But now the winds of revolution were strong, and Mouchette began to sense the first tremors of a collapsing regime. It was, perhaps, time to shift his loyalties once again, so that he would land on his feet when the government toppled.

Mouchette, after considering everything, decided that the person who would be best for him to contact would be Colonel Justin Barclay. He decided to send for him.

Justin continued to occupy his spare time in the same way he had since first coming to Vietnam, and that was by mingling with the people. He rarely went to an American officers' club or an American social function. He would go only if the function was a necessary part of his duty, such as command-appearance cocktail parties and receptions. And then he felt uncomfortable, because he was no longer able to communicate with Americans. To him they were totally blind to the most obvious truths, and discussions always left him frustrated with impotence.

So, during his spare time Justin attended the Chinese movies (with subtitles in Vietnamese and English) and cheered, along with the Vietnamese, when the sword-fighting knights dispatched the evil warlords. Afterward he would eat *my ton* soup and rehash the more exciting parts of the movie with the other moviegoers. Sometimes he would play *co tuong*, or listen to a strolling street musician, or watch a cockfight. It was just after an exciting cockfight that Antoine Mouchette's emissary found him.

Justin had bet on the winning bird and was buying beer for everyone with his winnings when a Chinese man approached him. He was dressed in fine silk, and he moved through the earthy surroundings of the small cafe with obvious distaste.

"You are Justin Barclay?" he asked as he approached Justin. He spoke in English, and his voice was apologetic.

"Yes," Justin answered. "Please speak in Vietnamese. I

keep no secrets from my friends." Justin gestured to the others, and they smiled at the honor.

"Your forgiveness, sir, if I've offended you or your worthy friends. *Monsieur* Mouchette, a gentleman of great substance and generosity, begs you to visit with him," the man said, bowing deeply. The words seemed to slide out of his mouth with well-oiled obsequiousness.

A general murmur of awe rippled among the Vietnamese who were present. They all knew of Mouchette. Stories of his wealth and of the fabulous luxury of his estate had grown into legend.

"His house is built of ivory, upon a foundation of pure gold," one story went. "He has enough rice in his storehouse to have a Tet feast for all the people of Saigon and yet not make a dent in his supply," went another version.

"Yes," Justin agreed. "I'll see Mr. Mouchette." Again, an expression of awe from the others. They had come to accept Justin as one of them. For him to see Mouchette was almost as if one of their own number had been asked.

"*Ong* Barclay, you will look at everything and remember, so that you may tell us what his house is like?" asked the owner of the cock upon which Justin had just bet.

"I will remember everything and tell you," Justin promised as he left with Mouchette's Chinese messenger.

"So, you are Justin Barclay," Mouchette said, extending his hand to Justin, when he arrived at Mouchette's villa.

"Yes."

"I am told," Mouchette continued, "that among the people of Vietnam you rank somewhere between Ho Chi Minh and Buddha."

"I am Justin Barclay," Justin answered, "but I don't plead guilty to the reputation you have described for me."

"You are being modest," Mouchette said. He led the way into a dining room, where a table had been prepared. Tamara was standing behind the table, and when Justin saw her, he almost gasped at her incredible beauty.

"The daughter of a dear friend of mine," Mouchette said easily. "She is Princess Tamara. I hope you don't mind that she is going to join us for dinner."

"It will be an honor," Justin said, staring at her unbelievable beauty.

"We'll talk after we've eaten. I've some information I think you'll find interesting. But for now, enjoy your meal," Mouchette said, motioning Justin to be seated.

The meal began with pate de foie gras, French bread, and a chilled champagne. Then a huge steak with Béarnaise sauce, a delicate rice pudding, and for dessert, Brie and chunks of fresh pineapple.

After the meal, they were entertained by Balinese dancing girls who were so graceful in their movements that they appeared to float on the air. Princess Tamara sat with Justin during the entertainment, making sure that his wine glass was kept full, and being attentive in whatever way she could.

Justin knew that Antoine Mouchette was going to ask him for something. He didn't know what it would be, but he had decided to enjoy the preliminaries anyway. He justified his enjoyment by remembering his promise to the Vietnamese to tell what everything in Mouchette's house was like.

Finally, Mouchette made a few motions with his hands, and everyone left, including Princess Tamara.

Only Antoine Mouchette and Justin Barclay were left in the room. Mouchette poured each of them a brandy, then held his glass to the light for a second.

"It's beautiful," he said, squinting through the amber liquid. "As if a bit of sunlight has been captured and bottled."

"Yes, it is," Justin agreed, waiting for Mouchette to make his pitch.

"To what shall we drink?" Mouchette asked. "Oh, I know. To a successful, and, hopefully, easy coup." He held up his glass.

Justin smiled easily. "I won't make a fool of myself by asking what coup," he said. "But I will ask, which coup?"

Mouchette laughed appreciatively. "Well, my friend, you are right there. There are indeed many men who have coup plans to which we could drink. General Don, General Kahn, General Dinh, your friend Big Minh, and of course General Tung."

Mouchette was well informed. Justin didn't reply, but he too held up his glass and drank as Mouchette did.

"Of course," Mouchette said as he put his glass down, "you know that General Tung is merely fronting for Nhu?"

"You have a reason for such a belief?" Justin asked.

"Yes," Mouchette answered. "General Tung has already solicited my support. He has explained to me that he is dealing with the Americans and that they are backing a coup. He has also told me that he is stringing them along in order to sow confusion and thus prevent a real coup from being organized."

"What did you tell him when he asked for support?" Justin asked.

"I agreed, of course," Mouchette said easily. "I thought that a coup would fail, as it has in the past. But now I think a coup will not fail. And I wish to ally myself with the winning side."

"I appreciate your candor," Justin said. "Tell me, of the coup elements you have named, which do you think will be the winning one?"

"I believe that an uneasy alliance can be worked out among them, at least for long enough to depose Diem. Afterward there may be additional coups, but the results will be of little consequence to all but the ones directly involved. The primary thing now is to overthrow Diem. America wants to do this, and I want to help."

"Out of dedication to the common good, I suppose?" Justin asked sarcastically.

"Out of dedication to self-preservation," Mouchette replied. "Will you accept my help?"

"Of course," Justin said. "I couldn't ask for a better motive. What sort of help did you have in mind?"

"I still enjoy good offices with General Tung, as well as with Nhu and Diem. I'll use those offices in any way you wish. Incidentally, I also exercise some influence over a few American officials, General McKenzie among them."

"You move in powerful company," Justin said. "So why do you approach me with your offer of help? Why not go directly to General McKenzie?"

"McKenzie has the title, but you have the *pouvoir*—the power." Mouchette smiled. "I have a talent for locating the person who can do me the most good—and you are that person."

"I am only a liaison officer," Justin protested. "I have no authority to act on my own."

"Perhaps so. But you alone among the Americans can communicate with the people. I know that you are aware of the general feeling about Tung and have tried to convince General McKenzie to withdraw his support from Tung. Perhaps you'd like me to try?"

"How would you do it?"

"General McKenzie enjoys the company of Princess Tamara," Mouchette said. "That provides me with ample opportunity to speak with him. I can be very persuasive."

"I suppose you could," Justin replied with a small laugh.

"Would you like me to try?"

"Not just yet," Justin said. "As long as Tung believes we are buying his act, there won't be any danger of him coming up with something else."

"That sounds like a good idea," Mouchette agreed. "But in the meantime, you will have to make alternate coup plans. Who will you make them with?"

Justin grinned. "Now, Mouchette, you don't want to know all my secrets, do you?"

"No, of course not," Mouchette answered easily, and not in the least offended. "But whoever it is, I'll stand ready to provide whatever assistance is necessary."

"Oh, and *Monsieur* Mouchette," Justin said, his voice suddenly taking on a more confidential tone, "there is one more thing. I'm approaching you on this matter not as a representative of the American government but as a matter of personal faith. I'd like your help in something."

"I'd be glad to help," Mouchette said.

"You haven't heard my request. You may wish to turn me down."

"Try me."

"I may want to personally guarantee the safety of someone. I'd like your help."

"Why, of course I'll help you," Mouchette said. "I'll establish contact with the American Embassy on this matter if you wish, and provide sanctuary until the embassy can get that person to safety."

"No," Justin said quietly. "You don't understand. I'm not sure the American Embassy would help."

Mouchette pulled a cigarette from a silver case and tapped it several times before lighting it. Finally, after lighting it and taking a few puffs, he looked at Justin. "All right," he said. "If you can get whoever it is to my warehouse in Cholon, I'll make the arrangements."

Justin smiled. "Thank you," he said.

THE CENTRAL FIGURE of all plans with regard to Vietnam, President Diem, was at that moment entertaining a group of newspapermen at a small reception. He seemed to be enjoying himself as he passed among the group playing the perfect host.

"My sister-in-law serves as my official hostess," he apologized, "but she is now on a world tour for goodwill."

"I had the pleasure of covering one of her talks just before I left," one of the reporters said. "I must say she's making quite a splash."

Diem smiled and sipped from his cup of tea. "I believe you are calling her the 'Dragon Lady' in your stories."

There was a small rippling of embarrassed laughter.

"I'm not offended," Diem said easily. "The name fits her well. Like the Dragon Lady in 'Terry and the Pirates,' she is a beautiful woman. And she is a powerful woman, of strong will."

Diem began to joke with the reporters, and they began to feel at ease with the little man in the white sharkskin suit. They started asking him questions, and one wanted to know how he felt about the United Nations discussion of the Buddhist question.

"I was quite surprised to hear of that," Diem said. "That problem has been solved to the satisfaction of both parties, and we are now down to the more serious business of going on with the war against the Communists."

"But there is a domestic crisis, Mr. President," one of the reporters countered.

"Not at all, not at all," Diem replied. "I admit to some general disturbances of a minor nature in the universities. But, of course, that is not restricted to my country, is it?" he asked chidingly. "However, all has been settled, and we would like to enjoy a little domestic tranquility—if the United States will but allow it."

"What do you mean?"

"I can handle my domestic problems," Diem said. "I can handle the Viet Cong if left alone. But I cannot handle the Americans."

The reporters tried to get Diem to be more specific, but they didn't succeed. He did discuss other things with them, and they were amazed at his grasp of facts and figures. He could quote aid statistics to the dollar. He also knew the tone and tint of Vietnamese support in the United States, and could name the senators, congressmen, and newspapers for him, as well as the senators, congressmen, and newspapers against him.

Outside the palace the shadows of evening lengthened across the city. With the approaching darkness the civilians, the police, and the army seemed to draw themselves into wary groups for security. They watched each other with suspicious eyes and prepared to pass another nervous night.

Big Minh was unable to secure a commitment from the other generals in time to affect a coup for the tenth of October, so he contacted Justin to plead for more time. Justin requested a meeting with General Tung, and Tung agreed. In keeping with Tung's tradition of selecting exotic meeting places, he had arranged to meet Justin in one of the small shops that serve as a folk doctor's office.

Folk doctors outnumber medical doctors almost 100 to 1 in Vietnam, but even if the odds were reversed, the folk doctors would still get the majority of the business. The average Vietnamese puts little stock in the simple act of dispensing pills or administering shots. To be treated for sickness, one must really be "treated," and medical doctors simply do not treat one. At least not in the way that the average Vietnamese can understand.

Folk doctors have a variety of treatments, as diverse as the illnesses they treat. Pinching, scraping, and pricking are three of the more common methods. One of the more exotic treatments consists of stripping the patient completely naked, then taking several small jars, burning an incense candle beneath the jars thus evacuating the oxygen to create a partial vacuum, and then sticking the jars to the body. The jars draw the skin up by suction, and the "bodily poisons" are thus presumed to be removed. The number and pattern of the jars depends on the illness and/or the patient's ability to pay. The jars leave marks, and some of the wealthier patients wear the intricate designs on their bodies proudly as symbols of their affluence.

A small wind bell tinkled with the breeze of Justin's passing as he entered the shop. Patients with various illnesses, both real and imagined, sat around the waiting room, much as do doctor's patients the world over. A nurse approached him, a look of curiosity on her face.

"I would like to be treated for vapors," Justin said.

The woman led Justin down a narrow, foul-smelling hall, and indicated that he should enter a small room at the rear of the establishment. Once he was inside, she dabbed copious amounts of chlorophyll on his forehead, chin, and chest, then bade him lie down on a wooden platform that was built alongside the wall. She lit three joss sticks, gesticulated in each corner of the room, and then placed them in a Coca-Cola can which sat in the center of the floor. They continued to burn, the fragrant smoke curling a path to the ceiling.

Justin lay there in total solitude for nearly fifteen minutes before General Tung arrived. The nurse administered to Tung exactly as she had to Justin, and lit three more joss sticks before she withdrew, leaving Justin on a platform on one side of the room and General Tung on a platform on the other side.

"Why did you wish to see me?" Tung asked. "Is there a problem?"

"There is a problem of sorts," Justin said. "I'd like to have the operation postponed for a couple of weeks."

"Why?"

"Something has come up," Justin replied without elaboration.

"Impossible," Tung said sharply. "I have the units in position, and the commanders are even now awaiting my orders to strike."

"General Tung, if you insist on going now, I cannot guarantee you American support," Justin said, trying a bluff.

"Colonel Rogers doesn't feel that way," General Tung said. "He is well satisfied with the time schedule."

Justin sat up quickly and looked across the room toward Tung. Was Tung trying his own bluff? Had he been in contact with Rogers?

"You've spoken with Colonel Rogers?" Justin asked, his voice registering surprise.

Tung sat up slowly, groaning with the effort, and let his feet swing down from the platform, where they dangled just above the floor. He pulled a package of cigarettes from his shirt and lit one, adding its stifling, heavy odor to the sweet smell of the burning joss sticks.

"I, for one, do not violate the agreements we have made," Tung said easily. "Our agreement was that I would deal only with you, and I have kept my bargain. However, Mr. Mot, Colonel Rogers' interpreter, and I enjoy a friendly relationship. Mr. Mot keeps me well informed of Colonel Rogers' feelings."

"Colonel Rogers is not always aware of all the factors involved," Justin said. "If he is pleased with the date, it is only because he is anxious for the success of the operation. As, indeed, we all are. But it is because I want to ensure success that I ask for a little more time."

"Colonel Barclay, as I have said, I have kept my bargain, and I have dealt only with you. Can you assure me of an equal fidelity?"

"General Tung," Justin replied smoothly, "your trust in me is as well placed as my trust in you."

Tung smiled, and a flicker of amused understanding flashed across his eyes. "To be sure," he said quietly. "To be sure."

"You will postpone the date, then?" Justin asked.

"Yes," Tung replied. "In fact, if you wish, I will allow you to establish the new date. I'll inform my commanders that we await the pleasure of the Americans."

"Thank you," Justin said. "Such continued harmony can only ensure our success."

Tung took a deep drag on his cigarette and looked at Justin through eyes that had narrowed into slits. Justin knew that Tung realized what he was doing, and he wondered if it was about to come out in the open.

Fortunately, the awkward situation was averted, because the nurse returned at just that moment and announced that Justin had completed his treatment for vapors. He could get an additional treatment to help ward off the return of the malady if he wished, but that would cost extra.

Justin was anxious to get out of the close, hot room and away from the heavy scent of Tung's fetid tobacco. And he was equally happy to leave the conversation, which had reached an impasse. He stepped back into the hall, took a deep breath, put his hands on his chest, and smiled at the nurse. "I feel better already," he said.

Justin had parked his Jeep nearly two blocks away from the folk doctor's office and was walking back to it, weaving his way along the incredibly crowded sidewalk. He sensed, rather than saw, a motorbike veer sharply out of the stream of traffic and come all the way over to the curb. There were two men on the bike, and the one on the rear was wearing a poncho. Maybe that's what alerted him, the hot poncho, even though it wasn't raining. Whatever it was, Justin realized he was in danger just in time to dive behind a small vegetable stand.

The edge of the poncho was stretched out stiffly as if supported by a ridgepole, the ugly, black snout of a carbine protruded from beneath it. There was a series of flat, sharp cracks as the carbine, which was on automatic, fired a whole clip of ammunition toward Justin.

The bullets smashed into the stand, chopping up a head of lettuce and exploding a tomato into a mess of red. There were a few screams, but the Vietnamese, already into a third generation of war, fell to the ground with the reflexes of seasoned combat veterans, and no one was hit.

A baby started crying and an old man cursed, but for the most part the Vietnamese just picked themselves up, looked around to see if anyone was hit, then, seeing nothing of interest, continued on their way. Justin brushed off his pants and apologized to the old woman whose soup he had upset.

Justin had gotten a good look at the gunmen, and by the time he had regained his feet and his composure they were gone, swallowed up by the traffic. But he didn't need to see them to have a pretty good idea of who sent them. Only Tung knew where Justin would be, so Tung had to have set it up.

It was obvious now that Tung had been aware of Justin's knowledge of the fake coup even before the meeting. So, Tung had decided to have Justin killed.

When Justin reached his Jeep, he spent several moments going over it before starting it. They might have attempted to buy some insurance by booby-trapping the Jeep, just in case the gunmen missed him. The first thing he checked was the wire screen over the filler neck of the gas tank. It hadn't been tampered with, and Justin breathed easier. A favorite trick of the terrorists was to pull the pin on a grenade and tape the handle down. The grenade would then be dropped into the gas tank. It would take approximately fifteen to twenty minutes for the gas to eat away the glue on the tape, then the spring-loaded handle would pop loose, arming the grenade. A grenade explosion in the gas tank of a vehicle is a very good way to kill all occupants.

After Justin had satisfied himself that the Jeep hadn't been rigged, he drove over to see Colonel Rogers. He knew that General McKenzie would have to make the final decision to delay the coup date, but he also knew that if Colonel Rogers wasn't pacified, Rogers would make it difficult for him with McKenzie.

He didn't look forward to seeing Rogers again. Rogers still denied having had anything to do with Nguyen's death, even though Justin knew it was a lie, and Rogers knew that Justin knew it was a lie.

The relationship between Rogers and Justin was like an armed truce, so they coexisted in mutual animosity, if not open hostility.

When Justin walked into Colonel Rogers' office, Rogers was standing in front of his desk holding the telephone to his ear. He looked up and saw Justin, then spoke into the phone. "Don't bother the General now, Captain, I'll get back to him."

Colonel Rogers hung up the phone, and then glared at Justin.

"I've got something I'd like to talk with you about, Colonel," Justin said.

"That's good, because I have something I want to talk to you about," Rogers answered, his words coming out in short clipped volleys, like rifle shots. "I was just about to speak with the General about you."

Justin saw the anger flashing in Rogers' eyes, and he knew that Rogers had already been informed of his meeting with Tung. He sat down and sighed wearily.

"How did you find out I requested a delay?" Justin asked.

"General Tung called Mr. Mot," Rogers said in self-righteous anger. "It would appear that that's the only way I have of being kept informed of what's going on."

"I'm not trying to go over your head with this thing, Colonel," Justin said. "That's why I'm here to see you instead of McKenzie."

"Perhaps you should be reminded, Barclay, that your job is not to formulate policy but merely to act as a liaison—a messenger boy, if you will—between us and General Tung. Now, by what authority did you request a delay? And why?"

"I have only the authority of General McKenzie, if I can get his backing. And the reason I requested a delay is very simple. If Tung moves on the tenth, the coup will fail. Not only will it fail, but we will be inextricably associated with the attempt."

"And what makes you so sure the coup will fail?" Rogers asked. He put a cigarette in his holder and lit it with the desk lighter. Then he wiped the lighter clean with a tissue.

"Because Tung does not have enough support. He hasn't recruited enough units from the field to make a coup," Justin said.

"Oh?" Rogers replied icily. "And on what do you base your information?"

"I know that there are many units that should have been approached. Their commanders are anti-Diem, and their forces are strategically positioned. Any logical coup commander would seek their support, and Tung has not done this."

"How do you know," Rogers asked, "unless, in violation of orders you have approached these commanders?"

"It's obvious that they haven't been approached," Justin hedged.

"But that's where you are wrong," Rogers said. He waved his cigarette in the air and looked at Justin with an air of triumph. "I happen to know that Tung has asked for and received the support of Big Minh, General Kahn, General Doung, and General Don. Forces loyal to Tung completely encircle the capitol city."

Justin couldn't keep the look of shock from his face. "Where did you receive such information?"

"If you must know, from Tung himself. And my interpreter, Mr. Mot, has verified it through direct meetings with the other generals."

"Colonel Rogers," Justin said, "that just isn't true! Mot is disloyal! He's in Tung's camp. Don't you know he tells Tung everything that goes on here?"

"I know Mot gives Tung a little information occasionally, but it is merely an instrument of barter, an exchange, to keep the channels of communication open. Mot is a dedicated patriot. And more than that, Mot is my friend." Justin sat quietly for a moment, and before he realized it, he found himself pinching the bridge of his nose in the way of the Vietnamese. Finally, he signed loudly.

"General Tung is not planning a coup, and he never was. He is merely throwing up a smoke screen to prevent a real coup from taking place. He is working for Diem and Nhu."

Rogers laughed mirthlessly. "Colonel Barclay, I must admit that despite my distaste for your misdirected energies, I find you fascinating. You have become so much a part of the Vietnamese culture and lifestyle that you have developed the same paranoia. You see plots and counterplots and assassins in every shadow. You've lost the ability to look at anything objectively. You are so much opposed to General Tung, for God knows whatever reason, that you will stop at nothing to prevent him from a successful coup. Do you really expect me to believe such a fantastic concoction?"

"I suppose I could really add to my paranoia if I told you he tried to kill me today, couldn't I?"

"Really? How?" Colonel Rogers asked with an amused chuckle.

"Shortly after I left our meeting two men on a motorbike tried to gun me down right on the street," Justin said, knowing even as he spoke that it was falling on deaf ears.

"Of course, the fact that there have been frequent, similar terrorist attacks against Americans couldn't mean anything?" Rogers asked sarcastically.

"These men weren't terrorists striking out against an American," Justin said. "They were working for Tung, and they were after me, personally."

Mr. Mot knocked lightly on the door and stepped into Colonel Rogers' office. He looked at Justin and smiled, then spoke in Vietnamese: "Don't be alarmed, Colonel, the shots were meant to frighten you, not to kill you."

"You know about it, then?" Justin asked, also in Vietnamese.

"Of course," Mot smiled.

"Mr. Mot, please speak English," Colonel Rogers complained.

"Forgive me, Colonel Rogers. It is so unusual for me to be able to talk with Americans in my own tongue that I couldn't resist the temptation to exchange a greeting with Colonel Barclay."

Justin stared at Mot for a few seconds. He felt as if he was in a world gone mad. He knew an obvious fact, and Mot had just verified it. But because America was both deaf and mute in this country, Justin would be alone with his knowledge. Finally, in frustrated disgust, he picked up his hat to leave. "I suppose you are going to fight against the postponement?" Justin said to Rogers.

"No." Colonel Rogers replied. "I was just calling General McKenzie when you arrived to tell him that we should go along with it. After all, Tung has already agreed to it, and it would not be good policy to let him know of any disagreements in our own ranks."

"Thanks," Justin said sarcastically.

"Besides," Mr. Mot said, again in Vietnamese, "We know you are negotiating with others. This postponement will just give us more time to learn their identity and their plans, so that we can stop them."

"Suppose I translated what you just said?" Justin replied.

Mot smiled. "Do you really think Colonel Rogers would believe you?"

"No," Justin answered quietly.

"I was just telling Colonel Barclay that General Tung wants only to serve the cause of justice and is willing to cooperate with the Americans in any way," Mot lied easily.

"But we Americans had best begin to cooperate

among ourselves," Rogers said, pinching the cigarette butt out of the holder with a tissue, and dropping it distastefully into the ashtray.

"To be sure," Justin answered dryly.

"Colonel Barclay, this is absolutely the last time I'll go to bat for you. As you can see, through Mr. Mot I have eyes and ears as effective as your own."

Mot smiled and said in Vietnamese, "Tell him otherwise, if you wish."

"I won't waste my breath," Justin replied to Mot as he left.

Once outside, Justin stood by his Jeep for a few moments before getting in. The street urchins surrounded him instantly, some claiming to have watched his Jeep for him and demanding payment, some already beginning to slap polish on his boots, and others simply begging for money. A pimp approached him and began offering him his choice of anything from young girls and beautiful women to young boys. One-half block down the street two wounded veterans, one missing an arm and a leg, the other missing both legs, sat against a wall with an upturned hat between them, begging. They were being totally ignored by the very people they had sacrificed themselves for. They alternated puffs on a retrieved cigarette butt and nurtured their bitterness as if it was a private affair, to be shared only between themselves.

Justin slammed his hand against the hood of his Jeep and then yelled out at those who had gathered around him. The anguish and frustration of all his years in the Orient came out in his yell.

"Get away, goddammit! What do you want from me? I can't do it alone. Get away!"

The kids and the pimps moved away quickly,

surprised at his explosive outbreak. After the initial fright subsided, they became angry and started cursing and taunting him from a distance.

"Fat rich American bastard! Go home! Go home you American bastard!"

Justin had heard that many times before, but this was the first time it had ever been applied directly to him.

## 22

A CLOUD OF CIGARETTE SMOKE HUNG IN A LONG LAYER over the conference table in the stuffy situation room of the Defense Ministry Building. The air was heavy with the acrid tobacco, and stagnant because the windows were kept tightly shut. The closed windows were to ensure the privacy of a meeting being conducted by the corps of Vietnamese generals who comprised the provisional junta. The meeting was to formulate final plans for the coup.

General Big Minh had listened to the discussion quietly, commenting only occasionally when a question would be put directly to him. General Don now had the floor.

"I think it is necessary," Don was saying, "that we elect a provisional President from our own number, and that we appoint him to that position now."

"If we do that," General Kahn replied, "it will appear to the world that we are ambitious men. That we seek a revolution merely to put ourselves into positions of power."

"Don't be naive," General Don replied. "Some sort of provisional government must be established. Surely you don't propose to displace the current government and then just leave it at that."

"General Don is right," one of the others said. "We do need to establish a provisional government now.

"Why not wait until after the coup? Then we can create a government composed of military and civilians, with the promise that general elections will be held within sixty days."

"That is a totally unrealistic point of view," General Don replied. "We will be unable to hold elections for some time to come. We can promise elections within a year, but I don't foresee any chance of that happening."

"Then what you propose is that we appoint a President now who will quite likely have a lifetime job," General Kahn replied.

"The country needs a strong leader, and a strong man needs a guarantee of tenure," General Don said.

"And you would be that leader?"

"If the task fell to me, I would gladly serve my country," General Don replied.

"What makes you think you are more qualified than anyone else?" General Kahn asked. "I have had a great deal of civil administrative experience, having been governor of the Northern provinces. I propose that I be elected."

There was a general outbreak of shouting, and charges of fortune-seeking were leveled back and forth across the table. Finally, General Kahn got the floor again.

"Gentlemen, there is one among us who is best suited. And he has proven his worth again today by not joining the parade of glory-seekers. I speak of Big Minh."

General Kahn pointed to Big Minh, who was still sitting quietly at the end of the table doodling on the pad in front of him. All eyes turned to Big Minh, but he did not look up.

"General Kahn is right," one of the others said, and there was a scattering of applause.

"I propose that we hold the election, and I nominate General Minh," Kahn said.

There was general agreement, and although Don's name was also placed in nomination, General Minh was chosen President of the Provisional Revolutionary Junta.

"Mr. President, would you take charge of the meeting now?" General Kahn asked after the election. "We've much business to cover, and it will go easier under your direction."

General Minh smiled at the others and accepted the position of responsibility, not with vanity, but with the confidence born of a feeling that such a position was his due.

"The first order of business is to decide the mechanics of the coup," Minh said. "What will be our procedure?"

There were several recommendations, as Minh found out, and each plan had its own proponents. Finally, after some of the more extreme plans were eliminated, it fell to a choice of three: assassination of Ngo Dinh Nhu, keeping President Diem in office, who would no longer be under the influence of his brother; encircling Saigon by the military, cutting Saigon off from the rest of the country and thus forcing a capitulation by the Diem regime; direct confrontation between military units involved in the coup and loyalist military units in Saigon. "We will discuss each of the three," Minh said, "and then select the one best suited. Who will speak for the first plan?"

"I will," General Don answered. "It is the quickest and easiest, and with Nhu eliminated, President Diem will be easier to deal with. He will listen to our demands then."

"Do you really feel that Diem could work with us after we killed his brother?" Minh asked. "I am not in favor of that plan."

"You are against the plan because you don't want Diem to remain as President," General Don spat. "You covet the job for yourself."

"General Don, you yourself are the one who said the leader we select should have a guarantee of tenure," General Kahn said. "I agree with General Minh. We would not be able to deal with Diem. For that reason, I favor the second alternative—encirclement and strangulation of the city, forcing Diem to surrender."

"That might avoid the bloodshed of a direct confrontation," Minh agreed. "But it would take a long time, and our coup must be swift and final."

"Then you suggest an attack on the loyal troops?" General Kahn asked. "Open civil war in the streets of Saigon?"

All the others looked at Minh. He returned their gaze with an icy calmness. "Yes," he said. "It is the only decisive way."

There was a general murmur among the group. Then General Don spoke. "Are you aware that the special forces in the city are loyal to Diem? They are an elite force and well-armed. There are many of them, and even if we defeated them, the battle would be long and much of the city would be destroyed."

There was a ripple of agreement from the others.

"I will talk to Colonel Barclay," Minh said. "The

Americans can get the special forces out of the city by merely telling Diem that they will withhold financial support unless they are in the field."

"Why must the Americans be involved at all?" General Kahn asked.

"Because, realistically, we can have no hope of a successful coup without American support," Minh answered.

"The Americans are committed to General Tung," Don said. "They are fools, and Tung is taking them in."

"Justin Barclay is no fool. He knows what he is doing. And Barclay is the only American directly involved," Minh said.

"You believe this man Barclay can get the special forces moved out of Saigon?" General Kahn asked.

"Yes," Big Minh answered.

The generals then agreed to Big Minh's proposal, and the method of coup was established.

The generals moved to their next order of business, that of lining up the participating units. They discussed troop movements and time schedules, and finally had everything planned to the last detail.

Then General Minh spoke again.

"Gentlemen, we are now at the most serious part of our discussion."

An expectant hush descended over the room.

"We must draw up a list of those who are to be executed."

## 23

THE GREAT OVERHEAD FANS OF THE MAJESTIC HOTEL turned noisily but did little to dispel the heat that hung over the lobby like an oppressive blanket. Justin was sitting in a wicker chair, a cold gin and tonic on the table beside him, reading a newspaper and waiting for Captain Phat, Big Minh's aide. It was just a little after noon, and Justin had the hotel lobby to himself, since everyone else was in the midst of the midday *ngu traua*, or siesta. Even the desk clerk dozed, stretched out unconcernedly across the top of the counter.

"Colonel Barclay?"

Justin looked up to see the scarred face of Captain Phat.

Well, you are right on time, I see," Justin said.

"Yes, sir," Captain Phat replied. "Are you ready to go, sir?

"Be right with you."

Justin drained the rest of his drink quickly, then stood up, indicating that he would follow. The battered old Citroen was parked against the curb, and Justin climbed in to settle himself for what he knew would be a ride without conversation. They rode through the streets of Saigon, now nearly free of traffic because of the noon siesta.

Justin looked through the window at the festering boil of Saigon's inner city. Saigon had seen its population increase almost tenfold in twenty-three years. The newly arrived people moved into one-room hovels with relatives who already lived in the city, or built little shanties onto existing structures, pushing out into the already crowded lanes and alleyways. Streets that were once broad enough to allow a double stream of cars had been turned into narrow, twisting labyrinths, barely wide enough to allow a walking man passage. Among these structures, and behind them, in dark, damp corners in the intricate maze of paths are the cubicles used for prostitution and opium smoking. Justin knew that there also was the spawning ground for rebellions—whether of the Viet Minh or the Viet Cong—or for plotting a coup.

The alleys are dark, even at high noon, because the overhang blots out the sun. There are holes and passages leading from one alley to another, and people scurry about like moles through tunnels, sometimes going for weeks at a time without ever seeing the light of day.

The car left Saigon and entered Cholon. Although Saigon and Cholon have grown into one large megalopolis, united under a common administration, they still maintain distinct and separate individualities. It is quite easy to determine the exact point at which Saigon ends and Cholon begins.

Cholon is the Chinese district of Saigon, and like Chinese districts the world over, Cholon has maintained its Chinese identity. In Cholon there are few outside influences, and whereas France had left its colonial mark on Saigon, there is little evidence in Cholon that the French, or any foreigners, were ever there at all. The overcrowded hovels that pock Saigon are absent in Cholon. Instead, there are rows upon rows of neat, spick-and-span shops stacked high with a variety of products. Indoor and outdoor restaurants are many and permanent, as opposed to the portable sidewalk soup stalls in Saigon. There are even playgrounds for the children, something which all of Saigon lacks. All the signs are in the Chinese characters, as are the newspapers, books and magazines. There is a theater on every block, and the marquee depicts some thrilling scene, such as a glaring swordsman holding a bloodstained sword in one hand and the severed head of his enemy in the other. There is nearly always a line waiting to get in.

When Captain Phat reached his destination, Big Minh met them at the car. He took Justin's hand and pumped it vigorously.

"Our battle lines are formed," Big Minh said. "We've agreed upon the question of organization and the method we will use. The units have been moved into position, and we are ready to strike."

"You will lead it?" Justin asked.

"Yes, I was elected," Minh answered. "General Don will be second in command."

"Is the junta really representative?" Justin asked.

"Yes. It also has some younger officers from the air force, as well as from the army."

"When will you make your move?" Justin asked.

"There is but one problem remaining. The special forces in Saigon are loyal to Nhu. If they remain, there will be much fighting. We will win, but there will be bloodshed. You can get them out of Saigon."

"How?" Justin asked.

"If the aid money intended for the special forces would be withheld pending their reassignment to the field, then they would be reassigned," Minh suggested.

"Okay. I'll see that it's done," Justin promised. "Minh, I want to ask you something."

"Of course," Minh said.

"What will become of Diem, Nhu, and the others?"

Minh stuck his hands in his pockets and turned away from Justin. He walked over to a tree and scraped at the roots with his shoe for a moment before turning around to speak.

"I cannot lie to you, Justin. A list was drawn up of those who are to be executed. The three brothers, Diem, Nhu, and Can. Colonel Doung is also to be executed. The council also voted to execute Madam Nhu, but it looks as if her life will be spared, since she probably will not return in time from the United States."

"Do you really think such a blood bath is necessary?" Justin asked.

"What I think doesn't matter," Minh replied. "It's the revolution. All will be killed, including the women. The children will be spared, Madam Nhu will be spared—by accident, since she isn't here. Madam Doung will share the same fate as her husband."

Justin felt his knees weaken, and he grabbed the edge of the fence for support. His face went white and his mouth dry. Minh was still talking, but Justin wasn't able to understand what he was saying. Finally, Minh noticed something was wrong and questioned Justin.

"What?" Justin replied, realizing that Minh was questioning him.

"Justin, what is wrong? You know the way these things are. Without this action, the coup would not be effective. The people would feel that Diem alive could still come back, and then we would never be able to establish control."

"Minh, why kill Le?"

"Le?"

"Madam Doung? Why kill her?" Justin asked.

"She is a symbol, and symbols are dangerous."

"Madam Nhu is even more of a symbol, and she will live," Justin said.

"The people understand that. She is not here. Madam Doung is here. She must be killed."

Suddenly Minh seemed to realize that Justin had a personal involvement with Le. He stopped talking and walked over to him and put his hand on Justin's shoulder.

"Justin," he said very softly. "Justin, forgive me. I do not understand your ways as well as you do mine. I didn't realize. You are fond of her?"

"She is not her husband and yes, I am fond of her," Justin said quietly.

"I'm sorry," Minh said. He held his hand on Justin's shoulder for a moment and then let it drop. Both men stood in silence for several seconds. Finally, Minh wiped his mouth with his hand in a gesture of frustration. "Justin, I can't change the decision of the junta."

"I know," Justin replied quietly.

"But if you could get her out of the city before the coup starts, I promise you her safety," Minh said.

"When is the coup to be?"

"We will wait for the special forces to be withdrawn from Saigon, but in no case, will it be later than the first week in November."

"Then I must move quickly," Justin said. He started for the gate, when Minh called out to him. Justin stopped and looked back at his friend, who stared at him in silence for a moment.

"Justin, a great deal is at stake. A word in the wrong place could—well, she is Colonel Doung's wife."

Justin glared at Minh, his expression a cross between hurt and anger.

"Forgive me," Minh said. "I know you wouldn't. Please feel free to use Captain Phat in whatever way you may find useful to help you save Le."

Justin let a smile return to his face. He realized that he had placed his friend in a difficult position, and yet Minh was steadfastly demonstrating his loyalty. He stepped back across the open yard and took Minh's hand, holding it in a strong, friendly grasp.

"We are approaching difficult times, my friend," Minh said. "Many of us will walk *une rue sans joie* before these times have ended."

"A street without joy, yes," Justin replied.


As Justin returned to Saigon, he wondered how he would best be able to guarantee Le's safety without compromising the operation. He decided the best thing to do was to let her stay in My Tho, and even to make no effort to see her, as it might disclose her location to people who might mean her harm. Justin felt reasonably sure that if she was not in Saigon at the time of the actual coup, she might be spared.

The city had arisen from its midday slumber, and like some giant jungle cat just awakening, it stretched and preened and scratched as it came back to life.

Housewives were beginning to shop for the evening meal, merchants returned to their trade, and once again taxis and cyclos filled the streets. Motorbikes darted in and out of the traffic, many of them driven by women, sitting straight and prim, their colorful *ao dai* streaming out behind them.

Justin had a strong sense of rushing—individuals rushing here and there, each interested in his own sphere, while all the time they were all rushing in, unknowingly, toward their collective destiny.

## 24

In My Tho on the morning of the day Le decided to return to Saigon, she got up with the sun and walked through the quiet house, picking her way carefully through the sleepers whose straw mats were strewn about on the floor. She stood on the open porch and looked out toward the Mekong. A soft breeze blowing off the river carried with it a fish smell that was somehow reassuring—as if reminding Le of the timelessness of Vietnam.

The fishermen of the village had already gone out, and their flat boats glided effortlessly through the still water, the reflection of the painted eyes on the boats glaring back from the mirrored surface. The clacks of the wooden blocks the fishermen slapped together to attract the fish rolled across the water with a rhythmic, almost musical quality.

Most of the predawn mist had been burned away by the red disc of the rising sun, but enough remained to clothe the scene in a diaphanous haze, making it appear as if the village were a painting on silk in pastel blues, purples, and rose.

As the morning shadows lightened, Le became aware that she was not alone on the porch. The father of her sister's husband was also there. He was sitting quietly at the other end, looking at Le with deep, dark eyes.

"The sunrise is very beautiful," Le said, startled by his presence and speaking merely to overcome her awkwardness.

The old man didn't answer. "I was unable to sleep," she added. Still no answer.

"It was hot, and I came for a breath of fresh air." Le was very uncomfortable, and the more she tried to cover her embarrassment, the more obvious it became.

"You are returning to Saigon?"

"Yes."

"It may not be safe for you there."

"Why do you say that?"

"It may not be safe," the old man said again, without clarification.

The sounds of the others awakening reached the porch. The private conversation between Le and the old man halted, and their relationship changed as abruptly as the closing of a door. He became once again the extra house guest, the old grandfather waiting to die. And she became the almost feared lady from Saigon, a relative by blood but a stranger by lifestyle. The temporary bridge they had built between them was gone. It was as if they had never spoken a word this morning. And now there would be no more real communication between them, only superficial conversation. Not even their eyes would exchange an awareness of the brief encounter they had shared.

"I have decided to return to Saigon," Le told her sister

when her sister stepped outside the house to join her on the porch.

"When will you go?" Le's sister asked.

"This morning," Le replied. "I will leave this morning."

Le had not gotten over the sorrow of her father's death, but she no longer blamed Justin for it. In fact, during her reasoning process she had realized that she was just as guilty as Justin. She had set up the meeting, and she had known that her father was a member of the National Liberation Front. And her father, choosing to immerse himself in such activities, had charted his own course long before. He was the master of his own destiny. There was no justification for her anger with Justin, nor for self-blame.

It was, Le decided with fatalistic acceptance, political, and Le had long ago decided to steer clear of politics. She would support orphanages, and help the victims of government repression, such as the villagers of Hoa Ginh, but that was humanitarian, not political.

Le was unable to hire a car to take her back to Saigon, and she had to go by bus. It was a fantastically arduous trip.

There were very nearly one hundred people on the bus, including the ones who dangled out the windows and those who rode standing on the back bumper, hanging onto whatever they could grab hold of. The top of the bus was heavily laden with personal belongings of the passengers—boxes, baskets, a bicycle, a sewing machine, a cluster of chickens tied together by their legs, a couple of goats lying down calmly, unsurprised by anything that happened to them.

Even the driver had to share his seat, and he had to fight with the passenger for room to drive, while the passenger, who was a paying customer, considered that he had as much right to a seat as the driver, fought back.

An old woman sitting between Le and the window suddenly climbed through the window and up onto the top of the bus. After a moment she returned, climbing back in the window and reclaiming her position, although the crowd inside the bus, following the principle of hydraulics, had expanded to fill her gap as soon as she had left. The purpose of the old woman's trip was clear as soon as she returned. She had gone for something to eat, and she sat there eating a raw turnip.

Finally, thankfully, the trip ended, and the bus pulled into the terminal on the docks at the river in Saigon. Le hailed a taxi, anxious to get away from the terminal and the reminder of the hectic trip.

As she rode through the streets of Saigon the tenseness of the city was obvious, even to her. There was almost a smell to the pending coup, as it hung in the air, like the odor of a heavy electric charge. Sounds seemed amplified and stillness magnified. It was not the same city she had left. There had been tension then, but there had been activity too. Student flare-ups, protests, strikes, reprisals, but each act seemed to work like a relief valve, venting off just enough pressure to keep the lid from blowing off. Now, however, Le could almost sense the pressure building, building, toward an explosion. And, for the first time, she was frightened.

Le noticed something different about the house as soon as she got out of the taxi. It seemed almost dead. She stepped through the gate and walked past the garden. There was no breeze, and wind bells hung mute in the still trees as if unwilling to disturb the solitude.

"Hello, Lan?" Le called. "Lan I'm back."

Lan was one of the servants, and Le thought it very

strange that Lan didn't meet her. She walked through the garden calling for another of the servants, and then for anyone, but no one answered.

The hush she had experienced in the garden was even more pronounced in the house. The rooms all stood in silent shadows, as no blinds had been opened. The ticking of the large European clock that stood in the hall was the only sound, and its chimes echoed hollowly through the empty rooms.

Or were they empty? A sudden sound brought an exclamation of fright from Le, and she spun around to see a man standing in a doorway. What little light there was, was streaming in from the room beyond the doorway, so that the figure was visible only in silhouette. Its sudden appearance frightened Le, and she stepped back with a gasp.

"Surely my wife has not forgotten her husband so soon?" Doung asked, stepping out of the door so that Le could see him.

"Doung," Le said. "You startled me." She looked around the house. "Where is everyone?"

"By 'everyone' I assume you mean the servants. They, like the proverbial rats, have deserted the sinking ship," Doung said. He took a drink, and then Le noticed for the first time that he was a carrying a bottle in one hand and a glass in the other.

"Doung! What are you doing? Why are you drinking like that? And why did everyone leave?"

"They don't want to be here when they come for us. Perhaps you'd like a drink? It helps one to face the inevitable." Doung held the bottle out to Le, who turned away in distaste.

"No? Well, no matter," Doung said easily, taking the bottle back. "It will be that much more for me, and I want it. I'm not blessed with the purity of innocence, which is your shield against such unpleasantness."

"Doung, what are you talking about? You are beginning to frighten me. When who comes for us?"

Doung finished what was in his glass, and then wiped the back of his hand across his mouth. "That's always been your biggest problem, my dear. You've never kept up with events. You should have, you know. There's about to be a coup. A revolution. Those who are out want in. Those who are in will be thrown out. We, my dear wife, are in. We will be thrown out."

"A—a coup?" Le asked. "No, you must be mistaken. The Americans wouldn't allow it. Colonel Barclay—does he know about it?" But even as Le spoke she realized that this was the tension she had felt when she returned to Saigon.

"Does Barclay know about it?" Doung asked with a short mirthless laugh. "My dear, he's planned it."

"Well, then, I'm sure everything is going to be all right. The Americans will arrange some sort of accommodation. They are against violence."

Doung laughed. He sloshed more liquor into his glass, then tossed it down with a flick of his wrist and a bob of his head.

"Doung, the Americans—they won't let anyone be hurt, will they?" Le asked anxiously. When Doung just looked at her, she asked again, "Will they?"

"No doubt the execution list has already been drawn up," Doung said matter-of-factly. "I imagine that Diem, Nhu, their brother Can, are all on it. They will be killed. I am quite sure that I am on the list too," he added, as he poured himself another drink. He stared at Le as he drank, watching her reaction, but Le stood mute. "Oh,"

Doung added, as if in an afterthought, "you are also on that list, I'm sure."

"What? No, that isn't possible!" Le gasped.

"Well, now, you really do need a drink," Doung said with a small chuckle.

Le shook her head no, and stared at Doung in surprise

"I'm going to the Continental Hotel now to speak with Colonel Barclay. I'm going to advise him of the foolishness of the American support for such an operation. I'm going to remind him that blood will run in the streets if such a plan is carried out."

"He won't listen to you," Le said. "If Justin has made up his mind that what he is doing is best for the country, you will never make him change it."

"Oh," Doung said with a confident smile, "I think perhaps he'll listen to me. Particularly if I remind him that some of the blood running in the street will be yours."

"And yours," Le replied. "Don't forget that some of the blood will be yours."

"To be sure," Doung replied. He smiled then took another deep drink. "Oh, I'm sure my death will be a glorious spectacle.

## 25

INSIDE THE CONTINENTAL HOTEL, GOSSIP WAS AT A FEVER pitch. Justin had not been there long before he heard the names of the coup leaders mentioned. He was finishing his drink when one of the waiters approached him.

"Pardon me, Colonel, but Monsieur Mouchette asks if you would join him?" the waiter said, bowing apologetically for his intrusion.

Justin looked in the direction indicated by the waiter and saw Antoine Mouchette, who smiled and waved to him.

"There is talk of nothing but the coup," Antoine said when Justin joined him.

"I must admit that we seem to have lost our element of surprise," Justin replied.

Mouchette leaned across the table, as if by this action to draw Justin into his confidence. "You have placed your support wisely though, because the coup will be a successful one. Even General Tung knows this." Antoine leaned back in his chair and smiled broadly. "I imagine you can look on this with a great deal of pride."

Justin glared at Antoine. "I take no pride in what I have done," he said shortly.

Mouchette pursed his lips, and a look of mild surprise crossed his face. "Oh? But aren't you and the other Americans making the world safe for democracy?" he asked, his accent putting emphasis on the "de" in "democracy," so that the word fell from his tongue like a challenge. "Surely your tradition of white hats and blazing six-guns will save the day," he continued.

"Mouchette, I've no wish to defend the actions of the United States," Justin said quietly. "And certainly not to a citizen of the country that has raped Southeast Asia through three generations of colonization!"

"Touché," Antoine replied. "But I'm not sensitive, because I have no loyalties. Remember me? I am a friend to everyone."

Suddenly Justin remembered that he had once asked Mouchette to help him provide safety for someone. Even then he had a feeling that Le might be in danger. Now he knew she was. "Mouchette, your offer of sanctuary still holds?" he asked.

Mouchette looked around quickly. "You may use one of my warehouses in Cholon, as I said. But only briefly. And I don't want to know who it is."

"Thank you," Justin replied sincerely.

"Well, well, my American counterpart and advisor, Colonel Justin Barclay," a voice suddenly said, and Justin looked up to see Doung, who had just entered. Doung reeked of alcohol, and his uniform, which normally was neat and crisp, was soiled. He was weaving slightly.

"Hello, Doung," Justin said, offering him a chair.

"Do you mind if I sit?" Doung asked. "After all, I'm only Vietnamese and may not be welcome here," he added with a slur.

"Colonel Doung, have I ever displayed ill manners toward you?" Antoine asked easily.

"Oh, no, of course not," Doung answered. "Nor has my esteemed colleague and fellow officer, Colonel Justin Barclay. But we all know how he feels about me, don't we, Colonel?"

"Colonel Doung, you appear to have had a great deal to drink. I've not seen you like this before. Perhaps it would be best for all concerned if you would go home. You shouldn't be seen like this."

Doung laughed. "By whom shouldn't I be seen?" he slurred. "President Diem? Mister Nhu? Nhu's wife? They won't be seeing me, and General Tung is right now cowering somewhere, frightened to appear in public."

"I think your own pride would dictate a more judicious behavior," Antoine said.

Doung looked at the Frenchman for a moment as if trying to focus on him. "Pride," he said quietly and without the slightest slur, "is a luxury that a condemned man cannot afford. And, Monsieur Mouchette, I am a condemned man."

All three men were quiet for a moment, then Antoine coughed once nervously, mumbled a *"Pardonnez-moi"* and stood to leave.

"In a hurry to leave, Monsieur Mouchette?" Doung asked. "Are you afraid that I will ask something of you?"

"I have to attend to a few personal matters," Antoine said. "I'll leave you two to discuss politics. I try not to get involved in these things."

Doung turned to Justin and laughed a short, bitter laugh. "That is a perfect example of understating one's case," he said.

"Good day, gentlemen," Antoine said. He smiled graciously and left.

There was an awkward silence for a moment, then Doung spoke. "Colonel Barclay—Justin—we are friends. Comrades-in-arms. You owe something to me."

"What do you feel that I owe you?"

"Your personal guarantee that you will stop this foolish coup."

"Doung, I don't have that within my power," Justin replied.

"You could withdraw American support. Without it the coup has no chance."

"I couldn't do that," Justin replied. "Even if I wanted to."

"Are you proud of your handiwork?" Doung spat.

"Diem, Nhu, and the others—including you—have brought this on, Doung. I tried to tell you that after the pagoda raids in August, but you wouldn't listen," Justin said.

"We are all guilty and must pay for our sins, is that it?" Doung asked.

"Something like that," Justin replied quietly.

Doung smiled wanly. "At least you are not trying to insult my intelligence by insisting nothing is going on."

"There is no sense in continuing with a charade when you know what's happening," Justin said. "I cannot change my decisions, nor can I intercede for you or anyone else. It's completely out of my hands. I'm sorry."

"But are you quite sure of that?" Doung asked. "After all, I should think you would at least be concerned over my wife's welfare. Therefore, I feel I can call upon you to devise some plan that would assure my wife's safety."

"Perhaps you are overestimating the danger to Le," Justin said. "As long as she is not in the city, she'll be safe."

"No," Doung replied, smiling broadly. "You are

underestimating the danger to Le. She returned to Saigon today. And if you have some plan that would keep her alive, you'd better move quickly."

Doung then got up from his chair.

*"Tạm biệt người bạn của tôi."*

"Yes, good bye," Justin replied, knowing that this would be the last time he would ever see Doung.

## 26

AT THE POINT AT WHICH THE CHANDELIER WAS ANCHORED
a crack had started, and had worked itself across the
whole width of the ceiling. The crystal and brass fittings
were dirty, and even the wires leading to the candle-
shaped light bulbs were frayed. The decaying pseudo-
splendor of the presidential palace mirrored the
decaying regime of Ngo Dinh Diem.

Doung sat in the reception room of the presidential
palace, along with General Tung, waiting to make his
report to Diem and Nhu. The heat and long hours of the
day had sobered him, and he had changed into a fresh
uniform, so that he was much more presentable this
evening than he had been earlier.

General Tung lit a new cigarette from the butt of his
old one, which he held with trembling, yellow-stained
hands. Other than the initial greetings, he and Doung
had not spoken, although Tung looked up at him occasionally with eyes that stared fearfully from deep-set
sockets in a small skull.

Somehow, seeing Tung so frightened had a calming effect on Doung, and he was able to recall some of the pleasure of watching fear in another man's eyes. For a brief instant, he felt as he did when killing. A cold appreciation of the situation swept over him, and he chuckled softly.

"Would you mind telling me, Colonel, just what it is that you find so amusing?" General Tung asked, his voice edged with ice.

"You wouldn't understand, General," Doung replied. "I was appreciating the irony of the situation."

"You are right," Tung replied. "I have no appreciation for the irony, nor can I understand yours. A full-scale coup will be here within a matter of hours. Since the special forces have been removed, there aren't enough soldiers loyal to Diem to provide an honor guard, much less a palace guard."

"No soldiers, perhaps," Doung said, "but I still have my Special Police."

"And just what do you expect those draft dodgers of yours to do?" Tung spat. "Direct traffic?"

"At least they didn't become traitors," Doung said. "That's more than you can say for your army."

Tung didn't answer right away. Instead, he took a few more nervous puffs from his cigarette, sucking in the smoke audibly. Finally, he spoke again very quietly. "We're finished, you know."

"Yes," Doung said. "I know. Are you going to tell Nhu and Diem?"

Tung held the cigarette in his lips and squinted his eyes into narrow slits as the smoke curled up. He looked at Doung, as if begging Doung to protect his secret, and shook his head no.

"Ah, gentlemen, gentlemen, I hope we haven't detained you too long," Nhu said, walking briskly into the room. He was wearing a pair of blue trousers and a white short-sleeved shirt. The belt for the trousers was much too long, and the end piece flapped ludicrously as he walked.

"Not at all, Excellency," Tung said. "We were just going over a few last details."

Tung lied easily, and Doung couldn't help but admire the way he had put his personal fear aside in order to speak in such a confident tone to Nhu.

"Well, come, come, don't keep me in suspense," Nhu said. "What is the plan?" Nhu rubbed his hands together, and his eyes shone brightly.

Diem came in then, wearing his habitual white shark-skin suit. The jacket wasn't buttoned, and it gaped open, showing a frame considerably more corpulent than his brother's. Tung and Doung came to attention.

"Please, go on," Diem said. "Continue with your briefing."

"Well—the coup is only hours away," General Tung said. "That is to say, our fake coup," he added quickly. "There will be some movement of troops, a few Special Police stations will be bombed, the radio station will be captured—only temporarily of course, to give the illusion that a genuine coup is taking place—and then loyal troops will push the fake rebels back and the coup will be crushed. The United States will be discredited, and any officers who might really be planning a coup will be frightened into inactivity."

Nhu's eyes flashed with good humor as he listened to Tung outline the countercoup plan. "Wonderful, wonderful," he enthused. "My brother has been so

205

worried, but this plan is an excellent one and can't possibly fail."

"It sounds quite good," Diem agreed. "But I wonder if we need do it at all?"

"Why shouldn't we?" Nhu asked.

"Perhaps there won't be a coup," Diem said. "General Harkins doesn't believe there will be one. And I am certain he doesn't want one."

"General Harkins is not informed," Nhu replied.

"He is the top military man in Vietnam," Diem said.

"Lodge runs things," Nhu said shortly. "He wants the coup, and he shall have one."

"But I'm certain that concessions could still be made that would prevent a coup," Diem stated firmly.

"And would one of the concessions include getting rid of me?" Nhu asked sharply.

"You are the greatest stumbling block in the way of harmony," Diem said quietly.

Nhu's eyes flashed in anger for a brief instant, and then he smiled, although the eyes didn't join the rest of the face in the smile. "You are my President, and I am a loyal citizen of Vietnam. I will do whatever you wish, my brother." He gave a half bow.

"General Tung," Diem said. "What do you think? Can we avoid a coup by making concessions?"

"Perhaps if we had made them a week ago," Tung answered. "I don't think we can avoid it now. I fear it has gone too far."

"And you think this plan of yours is the answer?"

Tung's hands shook as he pulled out another cigarette, and he lit it and sucked audibly before he was able to answer Diem.

"If we don't pull this thing off within the next twenty-four hours, we won't get the chance."

"And you, Colonel Doung," Diem said, turning to Doung. "Now that the special forces are gone, you have the largest single contingent protecting us. Could your police hold off a coup if a real one were to develop?"

"I am sure they could, Mr. President," Doung said. "But I think General Tung's plan has a much better chance of working."

"Unfortunately, my brother, we cannot afford the luxury of waiting to implement General Tung's plan when a coup starts. It is not something that you can fall back on. It must be put into operation immediately," Nhu said.

Diem pinched the bridge of his nose and sighed audibly. "Very well," Diem said. "You may put into operation this phony coup."

"Thank you, Mr. President," Tung replied.

Diem put his hand on Tung's shoulder. "No, General, I thank you."

Tung looked down at his feet and coughed nervously, while Doung smiled.

"You know, Diem," Nhu said cunningly, "this means you have burned your bridges to the Americans in so far as an appeasement is concerned. You are forcing their band, and they'll have no right to make further demands of you."

"Afterwards I may take a closer look at your position, just the same," Diem said just before he left the room.

Nhu looked at his departing brother with his mouth open in shock. Finally, after a few seconds, he turned back to Tung and Doung. Doung thought it rather prophetic that a few weeks earlier he would have been greatly embarrassed to witness such a scene between the two most powerful men in the country. Now the scene was academic. Nhu and Diem were no longer the powerful men they once were, and the argument was little more important than a family squabble.

"My brother is under a great strain," Nhu said awkwardly. "We all are."

Neither Tung nor Doung answered, and Nhu left.

"I must admit," Doung said after Nhu had left, "that for a moment you almost had me believing you. It sounds quite plausible. Too bad it's not going to work."

"It's not even going to be tried," Tung said.

"Why not?" Doung asked.

Tung was already lighting another cigarette.

"Because I can't even find enough troops to pull it off."

"Well, what are you going to do?"

"I'll be making my departure from the scene tonight," Tung said. "You should make your own arrangements."

At the sudden reminder of his personal involvement the almost euphoric appreciation of the death drama fell away, and Doung became once more a man resigned to his fate.

"Tung, do you have a plan for your escape?"

Tung smiled wanly. "Oh, yes," he said. "I have an excellent plan. One that is absolutely foolproof."

"How? What are you going to do?"

"Find peace," Tung answered.

"Take me with you," Doung pleaded.

"I can't do that," Tung said. "You'll have to take yourself."

"I—I'll have to take myself? I don't understand."

"You will shortly," Tung said. He started to leave, then looked back at Doung, and then around the room. "You know, the only good thing about this entire business is the happy fact that I'll never have to look at another one of Madam Nhu's gun girls."

Doung left right behind General Tung, wondering what Tung had meant by his strange statements. But never mind what Tung meant. The more important question was, what would he, Doung, do? Would he be able to die bravely? How he wanted assurance that his death would be a glorious one.

Without planning it, Doung seemed to find himself in front of a Buddhist temple. He walked up the steps and stood for a moment outside the massive doors. He knew that his acquaintances who were Catholic held close the Christian promise of life everlasting. A resurrection after death. It was a comforting thought to them, and even though Doung knew that it was a false hope, he felt cheated that his religion didn't give him the same comfort.

But surely there is some solace, some inner strength, which would prepare a man for death, Doung thought. After all, he had watched the bonzes accept death stoically. And, of course, those monks who had committed suicide by fire. What about them? They were certainly prepared to meet death. They sat there being consumed by the flames, and some of them had a serene expression on their faces. What was their source of comfort?

Doung stepped inside. The smoke from burning joss sticks had filled the air with a heavy, sweet aroma. On the far side of the smoothly tiled floor, two very young bonzes sat cross-legged in meditation. There was no sound other than the hollow thump of a door being closed in some far side of the building.

The differences between the Catholic Church and the Buddhists were immediately apparent, Doung thought. When he had entered a Catholic Church with his Catholic friends, they had been greeted at the door by aggressive priests who seemed desperate to win converts, as if keeping some type of score. Buddhists are satisfied that the true believers will come, and there is no need in their philosophy to win over nonbelievers. Therefore, one who enters a Buddhist temple must find his own way.

But Doung felt the need to talk to someone. He knew of the Catholic way of confession. Through confession, he had been told, one could find inner peace. And that was what Doung most wanted now. Inner peace.

He walked through the building, listening to the echo of his own footsteps. Finally, he saw an old monk, a very old man, sitting quietly. Surely a monk as old as he would have some comforting words to say.

Doung started to walk up to him and address him, but suddenly remembered that he was here to seek help and not in an official capacity. He stopped about fifteen feet behind the old man, and then took the same position on the floor. He sat in silence for several minutes. At first it was painful to his legs, since he was unused to the position, which for most Orientals is a natural one, but for Doung, now, was foreign. But after a short time; the pain left, and although he couldn't understand why, a calmness began to come over Doung.

He wasn't sure how long he had been there; the jumble and jangle of his thoughts had stilled and a tranquility had descended on him. It was as if he was independent of time and space.

"When you arrived, your troubles were great. Now they are less bothersome to you, and you are finding peace. You would like to talk?"

The voice must have come from the old man, although as Doung was sitting behind him, and the old man did not turn around or make any move, the voice seemed to have an almost idyllic quality to it.

"Yes, shih," Doung answered, using a term of respect.

The old man turned around then, and Doung saw him for the first time. He gasped, and for a moment the measure of calm he had achieved fled. The monk was Vu Dinh Due, the patriarch of the Buddhist temple in Di An, the same monk Doung had arrested, and beaten, back in August.

"Please do not become agitated," Due said. "I hold no malice for you in my heart."

Doung didn't answer, but he found the words of the old man comforting.

"You are troubled because you will die tomorrow," Vu Dinh Due said.

Somehow the absoluteness of Vu Dinh Due's statement did not seem disturbing or premature. Because despite any plans to the contrary, Doung suddenly knew with an almost mystical insight that he would die tomorrow.

"You wonder now what comfort you can find from Buddhism," the old man said. "Perhaps the words of the *Cheng-Tao Ke* will be of some help:

*"Like the empty sky it has no boundaries,*
*Yet it is right in this place, ever profound and*
*clear.*
*When you seek to know it, you cannot see it.*
*You cannot take hold of it,*
*But you cannot lose it.*
*In not being able to get it, you get it.*
*When you are silent, it speaks;*
*When you speak, it is silent.*
*The great gate is wide open to bestow alms,*

211

*And no crowd is blocking the way."*

Doung thought of the words, not consciously trying to decipher the meaning, but instead, letting the phrases soothe his mind. Vu Dinh Due left, but Doung did not see. Others came and went, but Doung did not know. Doung had glimpsed Nirvana.

## 27

Justin poured himself a drink, and walked out onto the balcony and looked down on the city below. The jangle of street noises floated up to him, and he could hear the words of a song being sung by a woman as she sat on the sidewalk and rocked a baby on her shoulder. Motorbikes and cyclos sputtered and popped and trailed a blue stream of exhaust as they zipped up and down the street. The evening bread-woman was making her rounds through the narrow alleys, and her singing *"bun mae"* blended harmoniously with the lullaby the old woman was singing to her child. Barefoot urchins ran through the paths clacking sticks together to announce the soup vendors, and already customers were coming from their homes carrying their own bowls, their mouths watering in anticipation of the soup.

The door rattled and then opened behind him, and Justin turned to see Le come in.

"I wasn't sure you would be here," she said.

"What brings you here?" Justin asked, though even as he asked the question, he knew the answer.

"Justin," Le said, "there is to be a coup, isn't there? And you are part of it."

"I'm not actually part of it," Justin said. "I acted as liaison, but I had nothing to do with the formulation of plans."

"Are those the same plans that say Doung and I are to be killed?" Le asked.

"You'll not be hurt," Justin said. "I promise you, you'll not be hurt."

"But, I am on the list?" Le asked in a small voice.

"Yes," Justin replied.

Le shuddered involuntarily, then moved away and sat on the sofa. She looked at Justin with confusion rather than fear on her face. "Justin, why was I put on the list? I've hurt no one."

"I don't know why," Justin answered. "But don't worry. I told you, I'll not let anything happen to you. Nothing."

But even as Justin made the promise, he wondered what tomorrow would bring.

---

HE COULDN'T EXPLAIN IT. IT MUST HAVE BEEN ONE OF those senses which are rarely used but which lie dormant until they are called on, and then surface as required. Justin was fast asleep, and he had heard no sound, and he was not touched. Yet in the midst of his sleep, while his mind was at peace and his body was at rest, a sudden awareness came to him and told him to wake up.

He sat up in the still dark room and saw a figure standing quietly just inside the door.

"Colonel Barclay, it's me, Captain Phat," the figure said quietly.

"Phat? What are you doing here?" Justin asked.

"This is the day," Phat said. "General Minh asks that you come now."

"Today?" he asked.

"Yes, sir."

Justin got out of bed quickly and began pulling on his pants. "Has it started yet?" he asked.

"There has been no fighting, but the units are pulling

into position and there will be soon, I'm certain," Phat answered.

"Where is Minh?"

"At the Defense Ministry," Phat answered.

They left then, walking down the narrow stairs and out into the predawn darkness to invade the world of the morning people.

"I will not be with you," Phat said.

Justin didn't question him as he climbed into his Jeep.

His Jeep was damp from the rain of the night before and from the predawn dew. The engine started sluggishly, and the rim of the steering wheel was wet and slippery in his hand. His foot slipped off the clutch pedal, and it sprang back against his shin, causing him to cry out sharply against the smarting pain. Finally, he pulled out into the street for the drive to the Defense Ministry.

It was only a short distance, and there was very little traffic, so the drive was not in the least difficult. When he reached the building, which was only one block behind the Continental Hotel, there was nothing there to indicate that a coup was imminent. The guard at the front gate was eating a bowl of rice, and he didn't even look up as Justin drove by. Only after he had parked the Jeep and had gone inside the building did anything look different. Inside, in one of the conference rooms, several high-ranking officers were standing around nervously, while others were on telephones talking with the field commanders. Justin saw Minh and went over to him.

"Ah, Justin, good of you to come early," Minh said. "I was hoping you would get here at the beginning. This is the day Vietnam will be given to the people. It will be a glorious day in our history."

"Has anything happened yet?" Justin asked.

"Nothing of significance," Minh replied.

"You call the execution of a traitor nothing of significance?" a nearby major said. "I think that is significant. It
establishes our determination."

"Execution?" Justin asked. "Minh, who was killed?"

Minh sighed, then turned away. "I did not want to
trouble you with it. I think it is not good to start such a
blood bath so soon."

"Who?" Justin asked again.

"Ho Tuu-Quang, Chief of the Navy," Minh replied.
Justin thought of the last time he had seen Tuu-Quang.
He was always smiling, as if apologizing for his rank. He
was a dedicated officer in a branch of service that was all
but completely overlooked in his country's priorities. He
was a harmless little man, playing a game.

"Minh, why was he killed, for heaven's sake? He was
no danger to anyone."

"He refused to join us," the major said. "Those who
aren't with us are against us, and they must be
eliminated."

"This rather unpleasant fellow is Major Nguyễn Văn
Nhung, General Don's personal aide," Minh said.

"General Don is the greatest hero in the history of the
Vietnamese people," Major Nhung said smartly.

"To be sure," Minh replied dryly.

Suddenly there was a shot from another room
nearby, and Justin jumped, then looked toward the door.
He started for it, but Minh grabbed him, gently yet
securely.

"No, my friend," he warned. "It is much better if you
don't go in there just now."

"Minh," Justin said, looking toward him with shock
etched on his face. "Minh, what in hell is going on in
there?"

"In addition to Tuu-Quang, there were two more

217

senior commanders who refused to join us. The junta sentenced them to death as well. Their sentences were just carried out."

"My God, Minh, what have we let ourselves in for?" Justin asked, pinching the bridge of his nose. "If we have this much killing before the coup even starts, what will we have later?"

"Justin, this isn't the United States. You know our people. The only way we can be sure of success is to have a united effort. Failure now would be disastrous. Please try to understand."

Justin kept his silence and went with Minh into another room, a conference room, where a briefing was being conducted.

The briefing officer, General Don, had a large map of the city, and he was detailing to the other officers the disposition of troops and the avenues of approach to the presidential palace. Suddenly there was a commotion outside one of the doors, and Big Minh looked over at Justin.

"There is an American reporter outside," he said. "I think it is best that you do not let him see you. Shortly after this briefing I must inspect the assembled troops. I have arranged for a helicopter flight over all the positions. Would you like to accompany me?"

"Yes," Justin replied.

"Leave now," Minh said. "I'll meet you at the airport."

THE HELICOPTER WAS FLOWN by an American who had no idea of what the mission was for. He took Justin and Big Minh all around the city. Trucks were lined up alongside the major roads leading into Saigon, and soldiers, wearing the brightly colored scarves of their divisions, gathered near them. Big Minh and Justin carried on their conversation in Vietnamese, so they were able to discuss everything without fear of being overheard and understood by the American crew.

"In addition to these soldiers, we have won over the air force, and they will be providing us with air support," Minh said. "They will strafe the palace and the navy headquarters, as well as the naval ships moored in the river."

"Do you honestly feel that the navy will fight against us?" Justin asked.

"Yes. Even now they are preparing for us," Minh replied.

"Will they warn Diem?"

"It doesn't matter now," Minh answered matter-of-factly.

The helicopter flew low over the rooftops of Saigon as it returned to the air base, and the angry snarl of its engine and the flat staccato beat of its rotor blades made the people look up from the ground below. And as Justin looked at them, he saw the face of the city.

AT NOON ON THE FIRST OF NOVEMBER, ALL SAINTS' DAY, Diem prepared to take his lunch, as did much of the rest of the city. Saigon was quiet. There was absolutely no breeze, and even the trees along the boulevards were still, without the slightest rustle in their wide leaves, as if they too had joined the siesta.

At the Gia Long palace many of the presidential guards had stretched out for their nap, and inside, Diem and Nhu, as they did every day, were also relaxing. All of Vietnam was resting, catching its breath in the midst of the incredible heat—all, that is, except the thousands of soldiers who had gathered just outside the city. They were buckling on equipment and checking their weapons while listening to last-minute instructions from their officers. They formed pools of frantic activity within the sea of tranquility.

It was while Saigon slept that these rebel units began their operation. Troops of the Seventh Vietnamese Division set up roadblocks between Tan Son Nhut airport and the city itself, then started downtown. Most of the guards waved them through, not realizing what was going on, but a few saw right away, and tried to stop them. Their bullets bounced ineffectively off the armored cars of the rebels, and nothing even slowed them down until they were in the middle of Saigon, very near the Hotel Caravelle. There they encountered stiff resistance.

Doung was at the central police station, and he stood on the front porch and watched the tanks roll up the road, raking the buildings with machine-gun fire. He was wearing his dress white uniform with full decorations, and he stood there, feet firmly planted, holding a pistol leveled at the approaching armor.

"Colonel Doung, it's the revolution!" one of his policemen called. "It's started!"

"Form a skirmish line and prepare to repel the attackers," Doung called out.

"Colonel, we can't fight them," the policeman replied with a gasp. "We have nothing but pistols to go up against their tanks. We'll be slaughtered!"

A flight of airplanes roared by them, just above the tree tops. They were firing, and Doung could see their guns winking. The spent shell casings spewed out and rained down into the street, where they bounced and slid crazily.

"Look, we aren't alone," Doung called out, pointing to the airplanes. "They are supporting us."

"Who are they shooting at?"

"The ships!" another answered. "They are shooting at the ships in the river!"

The bark of answering anti-aircraft fire from the ships added its din to the already noisy battle.

"Who is on whose side?" one of the other policemen

wailed, and some of them waved at the planes, while others sought cover from them.

Suddenly a tank round exploded in the front of the police station, and one of the men was killed. A spray of machine-gun fire sent the rest diving for cover—all but Colonel Doung, who stood his ground and leveled his pistol at the nearest tank. He began firing, and the others looked on in awe as the gun bucked and jumped in his hand, and the spent cartridges were ejected from the back, tumbling, catching the light and hanging in the air for a second as if in slow motion.

Doung had left the temple the night before totally resigned to dying. He had returned to his house, put on his dress uniform, then reported to the police station, which he felt would be the first to be attacked. All through the night he had waited. Not impatiently, and not with anxiety, but with an almost religious fervor. He had had what he considered a religious experience during his meditation the night before. A sudden cosmic insight that told him that death at the hands of his enemies was the surest way to attain Nirvana. And he was determined that nothing would deny him that death.

But the rebel tank commander was impressed with the bravery of the officer who, dressed in his white uniform, had emptied his pistol against a column of tanks. It was in the finest tradition of *nham nho*—futile bravado. Such courage deserved to be rewarded, and he ordered his tanks to cease fire, and they rolled onto the front lawn of the police station with their guns silent.

The policemen raised their hands in surrender as the tanks clanked to a halt. The hatch on the lead tank opened, and the officer in charge, a young captain, stuck his head through. He pushed his goggles up on his helmet and looked at Colonel Doung.

"Colonel Doung, I am Captain Xa. Please put your firearm down, sir. You are a prisoner of the provisional military government of Vietnam."

"I recognize no such government," Doung replied.

"Please put your pistol down, sir," the young officer ordered again.

So, it ends here, Doung thought, and he was amazed at how calm he was. At how detached he was, as if he wasn't really a part of his body, but instead was standing to one side, watching. And there was an advantage to the detachment. Things moved more slowly. Like the officer's last sentence. It was as if it were on film, and he could run it through again, and again, and again, as often as he wanted, and as slowly as he wanted, and still no time had passed. Time moved with the speed that he dictated, and he found it delightful to know that he could control time at will.

"The pistol, Colonel," Captain Xa said again. Captain Xa looked around nervously and licked his lips. It was obvious that he wasn't quite sure how to handle a prisoner as important as Doung. "Please, sir. If you don't put it down, I'll be forced to shoot," he pleaded.

You can't shoot me, Doung thought, with a silent chuckle of amusement over the situation. You can't shoot me, because you don't know where I am. You think that is me there in the white uniform, but that is only my body. I am here—over here—and you don't even know it. Besides, if you shoot, I'll just step out of the way of the bullets. I can control the speed of everything.

Doung watched the drama unfold. He saw himself raise his gun and point it at the officer in the tank, and he was able to feel once again the old thrill as he saw a momentary flash of terror on the face of the young rebel. The machine guns of three of the tanks opened up as one, and the bullets slammed into Doung, suddenly soaking his clean, fresh, white uniform with a spray of his own blood. Doung wasn't aware of pain, but he could feel the weight of the bullets, and even though it was as if he was still watching the scene unfold, he realized that the red-splotched body that had been slammed back against the front steps and then twisted grotesquely against them was his own.

Doung could see the others looking at him—not only the rebels but his own men as well. Their looks were not of pity, or compassion, or even of hate. Most were of morbid curiosity, but Doung recognized a few whose eyes betrayed the sensual pleasure they were experiencing, and Doung was at one with them. They were the ones he could understand, and he wanted to tell them that he understood, and that even in this, his own death, he could experience an almost carnal satisfaction. But he wasn't able to tell them anything, because he was dead.

The rebels jumped down from their tanks and began cheering, and the civilians who were nearby joined in the celebration. A few of the police also joined, and the first strategic position had fallen. Now the rebel efforts could turn to the next important objective, the naval headquarters along the banks of the Saigon River.

The sound of gunfire had carried to the palace even before the telephone calls began coming in. Ngo Dinh Nhu had smiled, first at the gunfire and then at the frantic telephone calls. It was exactly as General Tung had told him it would be. The phony coup was developing just as it had been planned.

Diem sat in a chair near the long conference table and drummed his fingers against the polished mahogany top. "I am not sure that this is what you think it is," he said. "I believe it to be the real thing."

"Don't worry," Nhu said reassuringly. "The coup has obviously got to look real or it won't be effective. Remember, they still have to capture the radio station before they start having their forces repulsed."

"There seems to be a great deal of shooting," Diem said. "Besides, Lodge and Admiral Felt were here just this morning. Do you think they would come here on the very day they had a coup planned?"

"Perhaps you are right," Diem answered.

"Of course, I'm right," Nhu replied. The noise of the battle grew louder. Machine-gun and rifle fire seemed to be an almost continuous sound, and frequent heavy explosions rent the air. Some of the explosions caused the chandelier to swing back and forth, and the glass tinkled musically. And then one very large stomach-jarring explosion shattered all the windows.

"Nhu, this so-called realism is being carried too far," Diem complained. "Is it necessary that we destroy Saigon just to save it?"

A messenger appeared then. His uniform was torn and smoke-stained and his head was bandaged. He handed a note to Diem.

Diem and Nhu had looked at the messenger in surprise, and Nhu watched Diem as he read the note. Diem read it without comment, then closed his eyes and pinched the bridge of his nose, and remained that way for several seconds.

"Well?" Nhu asked anxiously. "What is that note?"

Diem slid it across to him. "The naval headquarters has fallen," he said. "And Admiral Tuu-Quang was executed this morning."

"What?" Nhu gasped, grabbing the note. "Impossible! Tung would never carry it this far!"

"Suppose you contact General Tung," Diem said. "Not

to discuss the phony coup plan, but just to find out if he has organized an adequate defense. I'm sure that even you are convinced by now that this is the real thing."

"Do something," Nhu pleaded. "You are the Commander in Chief of all the armed forces! Can't you give an order that will override those given by their officers?"

Outside the palace, in the inner core of the city, fighting continued. A few tanks and the troops still loyal to Diem moved into position around the palace and began returning the fire. The booming explosions of the tank guns smashed windows and bounced off the walls of the buildings as the firing continued. As the tanks fired, children would stand beneath the tubes, their hands over their ears to block out the noise, then they would fight over the empty shell casings.

Diem got through to the Defense Ministry and spoke with General Don. General Don had just called on Diem the day before and had outlined a proposal for a compromise settlement of some of the differences. It was the proposal Don had offered that Diem had spoken of with Tung, Doung, and Nhu the night before, when he hoped for one last chance to avert the coup.

"What are you doing, Don?" Diem asked. "I did not believe you would make treason against me? Against your country?"

"I am fighting for my country, not against it," Don answered. "Mr. President, perhaps you recall our meeting yesterday? You could have prevented all this if you had been willing to adopt a new policy."

"I'm ready to adopt that policy," Diem said. "Have it drawn up any way you like. I'll sign it."

"Why didn't you say that yesterday?" Don asked.

"I needed time to think about it," Diem replied.

"Now it's too late. There is nothing to be done," Don said.

"But surely you can still stop it," Diem insisted. "I promise no reprisals against the officers."

"I'm sorry," Don said. "I cannot stop it. It is not my decision; it is the decision of the junta. Perhaps if you spoke with General Minh?"

"I will not speak with that traitor!" Diem said. "I would speak with the other members of the junta, but not with Minh."

"You must speak with Minh if you are to speak with the others," Don said.

"No!" Diem shouted. "I will not speak with that traitor! He stabbed me in the back!"

"Then it's no good," Don replied.

Diem slammed the phone down in anger.

"What did they say?" Nhu asked anxiously. "What did they say? Are they going to call it off? Can you make them call it off?"

Diem looked at his brother in surprise. The man who normally had ice water for blood was now showing an intense agitation and anxiety. Diem had to try to calm him.

"They said it was too late for negotiations now," Diem said. "But our men seem to be holding them pretty well. As time goes on and they see that a quick victory is impossible, I think you'll find that they are going to negotiate with us."

"Time? There is no time—can't you see that?" Nhu yelled. He grabbed the telephone and dialed the Defense Ministry. "I'll call. I'll talk to them," he said in nervous excitement. "They'll listen to me. They have to. I'll make them listen!"

Nhu got Don on the phone. "General Don, let us now

call a truce, and you bring your fellow conspirators to the palace. Here we can discuss all your grievances and make concessions."

"It is too late for that," Don said. "We can only offer you safe-conduct if you surrender now."

"Just a minute," Nhu said. He covered the mouthpiece and spoke with Diem. "They've offered us safe passage if we surrender now."

"You don't believe them, do you?" Diem asked.

"I don't want to be killed," Nhu replied. "This may be our only chance!"

Diem took the receiver away from Nhu and hung up the phone. "That is not our only chance," he said. "They will never let us live. We will have to make our own escape."

"How?"

"I'll call the American ambassador," Diem said. "Perhaps he can help us."

WHEN LODGE ANSWERED THE PHONE, Diem spoke with the voice of one still in authority and unworried about his own fate.

"Some units have made a rebellion, and I want to know what the attitude of the United States is?" Diem asked.

"I do not feel well enough informed to be able to tell you," Lodge answered. "I have heard the shooting but am not acquainted with all the facts. Also, it is four-thirty A.M. in Washington, and the United States government cannot possibly have a view."

"But you must have some general ideas," Diem replied in a tone now less confident. "After all, I am a chief of state. I have tried to do my duty. I now want to do what duty and good sense require. I believe in duty above all."

"You certainly have done your duty," Lodge replied. "As I told you only this morning, I admire your courage and your great contributions to your country. No one can take away from you the credit for all that you have done. Now I am worried about your physical safety. I have a report that those in charge of the current activity offer you and your brother safe conduct out of the country if you will resign. Have you heard this?"

"No," Diem answered. He paused for a long time, fighting his anger with the man he was sure was most responsible for his fate. Then, with a forced quietness to his tone, he added, "You have my telephone number."

"Yes," Lodge answered. "If I can do anything for your physical safety, please call me."

"I am trying to re-establish order," Diem said. He hung up and looked at Nhu.

"The Americans won't help," he said. "We are on our own. Have you located Tung yet?"

"I have not yet been able to find him," Nhu said. "But I will keep trying."

Diem walked over to the window and looked out onto the lawn. He could see his palace guards scurrying about, darting across the courtyard, squatting low, holding their helmets on with one hand as they ran, the other hand holding tightly onto their rifles. He could hear the shooting and explosions from just a few blocks away, and the frantic, nearly panic-stricken voice of his brother, who was on the telephone.

After several moments and several excited telephone calls Nhu walked over to the window to stand near Diem. He leaned against the wall and held his forehead in his hand for a long moment before he looked up.

"Did you find Tung?" Diem asked, not looking away from the window.

"He's dead," Nhu said. His voice was very, very small, as if he couldn't accept the truth of it.

"Tung is dead?" Diem asked, turning away from the window for the first time.

Nhu was unable to answer, he just nodded his head in the affirmative.

"Has he fallen in battle? Did the rebels execute him?"

"No. He committed suicide." Nhu looked at Diem with confusion mirrored in his eyes. "He did it last night, right after he finished talking to us."

"I'm sorry," Diem said, putting his hand on his brother's shoulder.

"He knew then, but he lied to us," Nhu said. "He lied to us, then went right out and committed suicide."

"Except for the troops outside these walls, we are alone," Nhu said.

"The time has come for us to leave, while there is still enough fighting to cover our action," Diem said, turning from the window.

"Where will we go?" Nhu asked.

"To Cholon, to Ma Tuyen's house," Diem answered.

"Cholon? We'll never make it. All the roads are blocked, I'm sure."

"Call Father DePaul. Find out which road is the best, and we'll sneak out," Diem said.

Father DePaul, who had attended the elephant race with Diem, and was a longtime friend and personal advisor, provided them with the safest route to travel. A Land Rover was brought to the back of the grounds, and Diem and Nhu climbed into it, then drove right through the rebel lines without even being challenged. Their escape was so simple, and so easily accomplished, that later an elaborate story was concocted about a secret tunnel, in an effort to cover the blunder of the troops who had surrounded the palace. The Land Rover met an old French Citroen at a point near the Saigon River, and the two brothers, who were literally fleeing for their lives, drove unmolested to the house of a rich Chinese friend of Diem's named Ma Tuyen.

With the coming of dark a gray drizzle began to fall over the city, depositing the ash and soot of the day's fighting. The ring of troops around the palace began to move closer. They fired flares which burst over the grounds, painting the low-hanging clouds and the trees and the building facades in a devilish red glow. Artillery was moved into position and artillery and mortar fire rained high explosives into the confined area. The bombardment kept up for several hours, then a force of tanks and armored cars closed on the last outpost. They poured point-blank fire at the protective walls. Diem's loyal troops—who had no idea that the President they were fighting for had left—continued to answer with fire of their own.

A high explosive round slammed into one of the loyal tanks, and the tank literally came apart with flaming pieces arcing away from the point of impact as if launched by rockets. A second tank joined the first, and then one of the defensive bunkers was wiped out as the loyalists began to fall before the murderous rebel fire.

Then, at 6:15 a.m., after a night-long siege, the rebels called for a five-minute grace period to allow the President to emerge and surrender. It was now November 2, the Day of the Dead, another religious holiday. Despite the offer, the President didn't come out, because the President had left the palace almost twelve hours earlier.

The angry rebel commander ordered fire resumed,

and at point-blank range, cannons, machine guns, and rifles began firing into the palace, smashing what little glass was left, splintering doors, knocking great chunks of stone and cement from the walls. Finally, a white flag fluttered pitifully from the area of the remaining defenders, and the rebels, realizing that they had won, began whooping and hollering and firing their guns into the air as they dashed into the palace to tear down draperies, grab silver and china, and celebrate their great victory over Diem and Nhu.

The House of Diem had fallen.

JUSTIN HAD MONITORED MOST OF THE PROGRESS OF THE battle from the radio reports called in by the field commanders. He had been there when Diem had called.

Throughout the long night, sounds of gunfire rocked the building, and finally in the early hours of morning Justin heard cheers and shouts from the men in the communications room. He had left the communications room earlier to try to find a quiet place for a few moments' rest. He was sitting in a chair, leaning back against the wall with his eyes closed, when Big Minh burst into the room.

"Justin, the palace is ours!" Minh shouted excitedly. "The troops have surrendered; the revolution is won!"

"And the President?" Justin asked.

"He wasn't there," Minh said. "Somehow he escaped. But he no longer has any troops to defend him. We'll have no trouble finding him."

Someone called to Big Minh, and Minh shouted back down the hall to him. Minh turned back to Justin. "We're going into the palace now. Would you like to come along?'

"Yes," Justin replied.

Although it was still early in the morning, the streets outside were a bedlam. Literally thousands of Vietnamese were running, shouting, singing, dancing with joy. They climbed onto the rebel tanks and dropped flowers on the rebel soldiers, and they smashed store windows and began carrying away the merchandise. From all over the city loudspeakers began blaring forth American rock music, which had been banned by Madam Nhu.. Here and there burned-out vehicles still smoked, and several people were picking through the rubble of the destroyed buildings. A handful of mangled bodies still lay where they had fallen, and the spirited music and the jubilation of the masses was a grim counterpoint to the visible carnage.

When Justin and Minh reached the palace, it was surrounded by the cheering throngs shouting, "Freedom, freedom—long live the junta!" They were unable to enter through the gate, but one of the soldiers showed them a hole that had been blasted in the wall, and ducking through, they entered that way.

The palace was dark inside, as the electricity had been cut. There were a handful of soldiers walking around carrying candles, and the flickering yellow light caused shadows to dance on the walls. Plaster from the walls and ceiling covered the floor and furniture with a thick white dust. Justin went into the area of the living quarters.

In Madam Nhu's suite many of her colorful ao dai filled the closets, silk bedspreads covered the beds, and elaborate drapes hung at the windows. Her bathroom was in pink and black marble, and on the basin, Justin saw several bottles of expensive French perfume and cans of American hair spray.

The soldiers grabbed the loot quickly, and in seconds everything was gone. Justin couldn't help but picture the same scene happening in Le's house, and he felt a quick flash of anger at the rebel barbarism. He was glad that Madam Nhu was away, and he was thankful Captain Phat was protecting Le.

Diem's room was a jumbled mess. Soiled white suits were on the floor. The bed was unmade, and the room was littered with men's magazines.

Justin stood in the door looking at the room for a few moments, realizing that the man s life was wrapped up in these narrow confines. Minh came up then, exultant. "We found them," Minh said.

"Where?" Justin asked. "Here in the palace?"

"No. Colonel Thao got the information from one of the palace guards who overheard them talking before they left. They went to Ma Tuyen's house in Cholon. Come along."

Justin went outside with Minh, and they drove to Cholon with the red light flashing and the siren going. Amazingly, once they were away from the center of the city, life was going on exactly as it had every day. Soup vendors were busy, sidewalk carpenters were working industriously, and the average person was trying to get on with his average life, totally unconcerned with the life-and-death struggle of his government.

Colonel Thao was waiting outside the Tuyen house when Justin and Minh arrived, and he reported in disgust that Diem and Nhu had fled just before he had arrived.

"Do you have any idea where they went?" Minh asked.

"I'm afraid not," Thai answered. "But I'll keep trying to find them."

"We may as well go back to the headquarters building," Minh suggested, and Justin agreed.

DIEM AND NHU had left the Tuyen house just before Thao arrived and had taken refuge in the St. Francis Xavier Church in Cholon.

"Father Guimet," Diem told the French priest who greeted them, "we need sanctuary. May we stay here?"

"Of course," Father Guimet replied. He let them in, then looked back into the street nervously before he closed the door.

"There has been a rebellion," Diem said. "Many of my faithful soldiers have been killed. I have loyal soldiers but traitorous generals."

Nhu's eyes darted around the room; flashing with fright. He was unable to stop shaking, and Father Guimet put his hands on his shoulder to comfort him.

"How may I be of assistance?" the priest asked.

"Would you say mass for us?" Diem wanted to know.

"I'm sorry, I cannot. The last mass has been offered. However, you can make confession and receive communion."

"Thank you, Father," Diem said.

Diem and Nhu took a moment to compose themselves, then they indicated that they were ready. Father Guimet took them to the confessional, and they made their last, private peace with God. Afterward they took communion and then Diem sent his driver to call the generals and tell them where they were.

"Why?" Nhu asked.

"We can run no more," Diem said. "I will not become a hunted animal in my own country."

"But they'll kill us!" Nhu protested.

"They probably will," Diem agreed. "But we have made our confession, and we are at peace with God. I am ready to die, if need be."

Nhu licked his lips nervously and rubbed his hands together as if washing them. "Why do they want to kill us? Everything we've done, we've done for the good of the country. Diem—talk to them. Perhaps if you, the President, would plead with them. Beg them to spare us."

"It will do no good," Diem said.

"But why would they want to kill me?" Nhu asked. "I have no authority, no position. You are the President. I have merely been an advisor to you, nothing more."

Diem looked at his brother, not with a look of disgust, but rather of compassion.

"I'm sorry," Diem said quietly. "I really am sorry."

Diem ate a sweet cake while they waited, but Nhu paced back and forth in the rectory nervously. He continued to rub his hands together, and every few minutes he would peek through the blinds.

Finally, there was a sound of brakes and several shouts. Nhu stepped to the window quickly and looked outside. He saw an armored personnel carrier and two Jeeps.

"They are here," Nhu said, his voice going a full octave higher in his fear.

"Are there any generals with them?" Diem asked. "I won't surrender to anyone less than a General."

Nhu looked again. "Yes, I see General Mai Huu Xaun," he said. "He's sitting in one of the Jeeps. There are a couple of colonels too."

"The arrogant young Turks," Diem said derisively. "But it is good that there is a General with them. At least we will get a military execution and will be spared a lynch mob."

"Diem," Nhu said, "no one is watching the back door. We can still escape."

"Nhu," Diem said sharply, "pull yourself together. Now come. We will surrender like men, and as befits the position of a chief of state."

Diem and Nhu walked out into the light drizzle. Soldiers were standing in a half circle around the door of the church, holding guns pointed toward the two brothers.

"My, are we as dangerous as all this?" Diem said, taking in the armed troops with a small wave of his hand.

The door through which they had come slammed shut, and the noise startled one of the privates. He dropped his gun and let out a sharp exclamation of fear.

"Don't be nervous, son," Diem said soothingly to the young private. "We have no one with us here. You are in no danger."

General Xuan had not left his Jeep. He looked at the exchange dispassionately. "Bind them," he said simply.

"Wait a minute!" Nhu called out. "Is this the way you take prisoners. You might show a little respect for your President!"

One of the soldiers struck Nhu, and Nhu fell to his knees. Another grabbed him quickly, and they tied his hands behind his back.

"General, I protest the crude manner in which you are handling this," Diem said sharply. "I intend to make this protest to your superiors when we reach headquarters."

General Xuan smiled wryly and got back into his Jeep without speaking.

Diem was bound also, then he and Nhu were thrown into the personnel carrier and pushed to the floor. "This is uncomfortable," Diem complained.

"You won't be uncomfortable long," one of the officers said, laughing shortly.

"I know you," Diem said. "You are Major Nhung, General Don's aide.

"Nguyen Van Nhung," Nhung said. "I want you to know me,"

"Yes," Diem said, grunting from the strain of his uncomfortable position. "You are an appropriate aide for a traitor."

Nhung climbed onto the top of the carrier and shouted something. The engines started then, and the convoy left the church. Diem and Nhu were pressed together on the floor of the vehicle, and they bounced painfully as the armored car got under way. There was blood on Nhu's mouth where he had been hurt. He was biting his lip and blinking his eyes.

Private Jung Il Mot sat on the floor with them, guarding them with his carbine. He had never seen the president this close, and he felt a small thrill at being here.

"It is not a long trip, my brother," Mot heard Diem say soothingly.

Nuh's eyes reflected terror, and Mot was surprised, and somewhat embarrassed by that. He glanced away.

Nhung was riding on top with Captain Nghia, but shortly after they got started, Nhung jumped down inside. He took his pistol out and held it in Nhu's face, pushing the barrel against his nose. Nhu tried to turn his head away, but Major Nhung kept the pressure of the pistol against his nose. He pushed so hard that Nhu's nose began to bleed. Nhung laughed.

"When General Don hears of this, you'll be severely punished!" Diem said.

The vehicle stopped moving.

"What is it? Why have we stopped?" Major Nhung shouted up to Captain Nghia, who was still riding on top of the carrier.

Nghia looked down through the turret opening, and to Private Mot, from his position on the floor, it looked as if Nghia's head was framed by a halo, as the light was behind him. Mot could see him only in silhouette.

"We've stopped at a railroad crossing," Nghia said. "It won't be long."

"It will be long enough," Nhung said. He put his pistol behind Nhu's head and fired. The sound of the shot inside the closed vehicle was deafening, and if Nhu shouted out, his voice was drowned by the noise.

"You—my God—what have you done?" Diem gasped.

Nhung, still smiling, turned Diem over, then shot him in the back of the head also. Afterward he took out his bayonet and stabbed each of the now dead brothers several times, then began hacking at them.

Captain Nghia watched from his perch on top of the carrier and never said a word. Justin was waiting, along with General Minh, at the Defense Ministry headquarters when the convoy arrived. There was a general movement toward the APC, then a few exclamations of shock and disbelief when Major Nhung stepped outside. His hands and clothes were stained with blood, and he smiled, and unconsciously wiped his hand across his face, leaving a crimson smear on his cheek.

Mot, without being seen, dipped his handkerchief into the blood of his president.

"Major Nhung, what happened?" Minh demanded wildly.

"My God," Justin said, turning away.

"We didn't want it like this," Minh said. "They were supposed to be given a military execution—not butchered."

As had Mot, some of the other soldiers began dipping their handkerchiefs into the blood, while a few others shouted out cheers over the death of the despots.

An aide approached General Minh and spoke with him briefly.

"Excuse me, Justin," Minh said. "I must go inside for a moment."

Justin started to go with him, but Minh held his hand out. "I'll be right back," he said, making it obvious that he didn't want Justin to go with him.

Justin walked away from the cheering soldiers and stood to one side, watching. The APC carrying the bodies still sat in the corner of the Defense Ministry parking lot, and Justin could see a foot hanging out the back door.

Minh came back outside and stood on the steps. He smiled and said something to his aide, then he held his arms up.

"My soldiers," he called, "we have just been in contact with the Americans. They send their congratulations and assure me that they will grant recognition to our new government within a matter of days."

There were cheers, then someone shouted, "Long live the Revolutionary Military Government!"

And then they all shouted, "Long live General Minh!" Minh stood on the steps with his arms held up, smiling at the cheering soldiers.

Justin stood back quietly and looked into the face of

Big Minh, and into his eyes, which had an almost demonic glow. And for the briefest instant Justin felt that his old friend had suddenly become a stranger to him.

## 31

IN THE LATE AFTERNOON OF THE DAY AFTER THE BATTLE, A low-lying layer of scud hung over Saigon. The inversion had captured the smoke of battle, so that a heavy cordite smell remained in the stagnant air. Despite the lack of sun, it was very hot, and the heat was all the more oppressive because of the absence of a breeze.

Big Minh stood behind his desk for a few moments trying to compose his thoughts. There was one more thing he had to do. It was his duty, and it had to be done. He walked out to his Jeep, and when his driver stood at attention, Minh dismissed him, telling him that he wanted to drive himself.

He headed for Justin's apartment, where he knew Justin would be sleeping. When he got there and had climbed the stairs, someone moved out of the shadows toward him. It was Captain Phat.

"He is asleep," Captain Phat said.

"Where is Le?"

"She is waiting for me at her villa. I will take her to Mouchette's warehouse in Cholon, where she'll be safe."

"Go to her. Keep her safe. I promised Colonel Barclay that I would protect her, and I intend to do just that."

"Yes, sir," Phat replied. He started down the stairs, moving quietly.

"Captain Phat," Big Minh called after him. "Yes, General?"

"You are a good man, Captain Phat."

"Thank you, sir," Phat replied without emotion. Minh let himself into Justin's apartment. He could hear Justin's soft, even breathing, and knew he was sound asleep. Minh called out to him.

"What? What is it?" Justin asked groggily.

"Justin, it's me," Minh answered softly.

"Minh, what—what are you doing here?" Justin asked, sitting up. "Is something wrong? Le! Where is Le?"

"Le will be all right," Minh said. "Captain Phat has just left to take her to Mouchette's warehouse."

"Thank God," Justin said. He rubbed his hand through his hair and across his eyes. He laughed, a short, relieved laugh. "You had me scared for a moment." Minh did not answer.

"What is it? What's wrong?" Justin asked.

"I'd like you to take a ride with me," Minh said. "I need to talk to someone...to a friend."

Justin agreed. He got dressed while Minh stood silently by the window, looking out into the street.

"Anywhere in particular you want to go?" Justin asked as he finished dressing.

"I thought we might drive down to the river, then take a walk. I like the river," Minh said.

Justin followed Minh out to the Jeep, and as they drove through the streets of the city, they spoke of old times like two friends who had met for the first time in several years.

Finally, they stopped near the river and got out to walk along its edge.

An oxcart came creaking down the path, with an old man walking in front, leading the ox by its halter. The cart was full of sugarcane, and Minh bought a piece, cut it in two, and gave half of it to Justin.

They began peeling it and chewing it, spitting the pieces into the river. Minh pointed to a large oceangoing barge which was in front of them. A handful of men were working on the deck. They were wearing only shorts, and they looked weak and scrawny, but they were handling hundred-pound sacks of rice with as much ease as the huskiest stevedore in America.

"Do you ever wish you could just be one of those men?" Justin asked. "Just to have the peace and tranquility of a slow, measured life, such as theirs?"

"Yes," Minh answered. "I have wished it many times. But for me it is not to be. I have been placed here by events, not of my own choosing."

Minh looked reflective for a second, and Justin made a fist and playfully punched him on the arm. "Events couldn't have chosen a better man," he said. "How is the revolution going?"

"The revolution is going as planned," Minh answered.

"You did a good job, my friend," Justin said. "You were successful where others have failed."

"We could not afford to fail this time," Minh said. "The Diem government had to be removed."

"I just wish his removal could have been less violent. The brutal slaying of Diem and Nhu was not good."

"I did not want them to die as they did, but their deaths were necessary," Minh said.

"The execution list was drawn up very carefully," Minh added. "Everyone on that list was placed there because of the danger they posed to the new government. And all such dangers must be eliminated."

"And who constitutes enough of a threat to be on that list?" Justin asked.

"Anyone who might cause us harm. Even someone who might harm us unintentionally. Someone whose continued existence might dilute the purity of the revolution."

A group of children playing tag came down the path then, laughing and shouting, and they ran between Justin and Minh, separating them for a moment.

"There is our future," Minh said, pointing to the children. "I want them to grow up in a Vietnam that belongs only to the Vietnamese. A country that is free."

"You have given them that hope," Justin said.

"Perhaps." Big Minh's voice was low, as if he was speaking only to himself. "But there is so much to be done."

The sun was setting, and rose-colored fingers of light touched the water, painting it red.

The sun is just coming up in Washington now, Justin thought.

He stretched, then reached down and picked up a stone and skipped it across the surface of the river.

"I used to do that when I was a kid," Justin said. He laughed at the memory and turned around.

Minh had pulled out his gun and was pointing it at Justin.

"Minh—Minh, what are you doing?"

Justin started to move toward him.

"Why?"

"Because, my friend, yours was the last name on the list."

Minh pulled the trigger. Justin grabbed his chest, a look of shock etched on his face. Then he pitched over backward, and slid head down into the water.

Big Minh looked down at him for a short while.

"I'm sorry, Justin Barclay."

## 32

Le couldn't wait for Captain Phat. She was frightened, and she wanted to find Justin. The two of them had developed an unlikely friendship, and she believed that he could keep her safe. She was running through the streets of Saigon in a state of near panic. Where was Justin? How could she find him?

A cyclo came by, and Le hailed it and asked to be taken to the American Embassy. Perhaps they would know where Justin was.

It was dusk now, and the clouds that had hung over the city all day made it even darker. It wasn't actually raining, but there was a slight mist, and as she was riding in the open seat of the motorcycle, it blew against her face with a stinging spray.

The cyclo stopped in front of the American Embassy, and Le got out. She started to go inside, but the marine guard came to attention and brought his rifle up across his chest.

"I'm sorry, miss, but you can't pass," he said.

"I must get in," she replied. "I must find someone—a Colonel Justin Barclay. Do you know him?"

"No, ma'am, I'm afraid I don't," the young marine said.

"Well, I'm sure someone inside can help me," she said. "If you'll just let me go in."

"I can call the duty officer, ma'am," the guard said. "That's all I can do."

"Just ask for Colonel Barclay," Le said.

She stood there watching as the young American called. The phone was too far away for her to hear what was being said, but she knew from the expression on his face that Justin wasn't inside.

"I'm sorry, ma'am. The duty officer says he hasn't seen Colonel Barclay all day."

"Thank you," Le said. She returned to the cyclo, which was still sitting at the curb. Perhaps General Minh would know where Justin was. She would go see him; he would help her.

"Take me to the Defense Ministry," she ordered.

"Yes, madam," the driver said, starting the loud popping two-cycle engine again.

Le didn't know what would happen to her when she got there, but she didn't care. She had to find Justin, no matter what the danger.

The soldiers in front of the Defense Ministry building were all drunk, and were still drinking. They held bottles in their hands, and wore leis of flowers around their necks, put there earlier by schoolgirls who were celebrating the revolution. But the schoolgirls were gone now, and they had been replaced by the prostitutes and bar girls.

The prostitutes were all wearing brightly colored Western-style dresses and heavy makeup and false eyelashes. They were throwing their arms around the soldiers and propositioning them openly, and the soldiers were laughing and pinching them or kissing and fondling their breasts.

Le paid her cyclo driver and stood in the blue haze of his exhaust smoke a few seconds after he drove off, looking at the wild activity going on around her. She shuddered involuntarily.

A soldier grabbed her, and Le pushed him away and walked over to the gate, where two NCOs were standing apart from the others. They appeared to be sober, and there were no women around them.

"Get away," one of them said as Le approached. "I said we don't want anything to do with any of you people."

"I'm not one of them," Le said, pointing toward the prostitutes. "I'm Madam Doung. I want to speak with General Minh."

"I know—you're Madam Doung, and I'm Emperor Bao Dai," the first NCO said.

"Wait a minute," the other one said quickly. He looked at Le for a second. "She's telling the truth. She is Madam Doung."

"What? How do you know?"

"I know. I've seen her picture hundreds of times," he said.

"I'm sorry, madam," the first NCO apologized. "I didn't recognize you."

"That's all right," Le replied. "Now, please, may I be taken to see General Minh?"

"Yes, of course," the NCO said. "Come with me, madam. I'll take you inside and get an officer to help you."

The NCO took Le into the building and told her to wait in one of the anterooms. As luck would have it, he had gone no more than twenty steps down the hall when he saw Major Nhung.

"Major, guess who I have in the anteroom?" he said.

"I'm not in the least interested," Major Nhung replied.

"Well, I don't know what to do with her," the NCO complained. "She said she wanted to see General Minh."

"She?" Nhung asked, looking up for the first time.

"Yes, sir," he answered. "It's Madam Doung."

"You have Madam Doung in that room?" Nhung asked, now showing a great deal of interest.

"Yes, sir," the NCO answered. "And I don't know what to do."

"Never mind, I'll take care of her," Nhung promised, his eyes flashing in intense interest.

Le had waited impatiently. After what seemed an eternity, an officer finally came into the room. Le recognized him.

"Major Nhung. Oh, thank God, they sent me an officer I know. Could you please arrange a meeting for me with General Minh?"

Nhung, still flushed with excitement after having killed both Diem and Nhu, and still covered with their blood, locked the door behind him and faced Le with an evil smile.

## 33

IT WASN'T UNTIL LATER THAT NIGHT THAT BIG MINH found out that Le had been killed. He was told that she had come to the Defense Ministry looking for him, and then her body was found later, hacked and mutilated almost beyond recognition.

Minh talked to the NCO who had escorted Le into the building, and the NCO told him that he had informed Major Nhung of Le's presence. Another witness had seen Nhung enter the anteroom shortly after the NCO left, so it was obvious to Minh who had done the killing.

Minh had Nhung arrested and locked in a tiger cage cell. A tiger cage is a steel cage built into the ground, not tall enough for a man to stand in and not wide enough for him to sit down. As long as he is locked up the prisoner has to remain in a semi-stooped position. He takes care of bowel and bladder functions as best he can in this excruciating position.

Minh let Nhung stay there for three days before he went to see him. Nhung had been without food and in that backbreaking position for the whole time, and was nearly delirious when Minh approached the cage.

"Nhung, do you hear me?" Minh called out softly.

"What?" Nhung mumbled. "What is it?"

"Nhung, look up. Open your eyes. Can you see me?" Minh asked.

Nhung moved around as best he could and turned his head so that he could look at Minh. When he recognized him, his eyes began to plead with him.

"Do you recognize me?" Minh asked. "Do you know who I am?"

"Yes," Nhung mumbled.

"Who am I, Nhung?"

"You...are...General Minh," Nhung managed to say.

"That is good," Minh said. "Would you like some water?"

"Yes, yes, please," Nhung begged.

Minh walked over to a bucket and dipped a cup into it. He carried the water over to Nhung, and when Nhung drank the whole cup, then held it out for more, Minh filled it again and gave him a second cup.

"Thank you," Nhung said.

"Are you quite alert?" Big Minh asked.

"Yes, yes, thank you," Nhung said. Some life appeared to come back into his eyes.

"Ah, that is good, good," Minh said. Minh began removing his belt, and then he made a loop in it.

"You see," he said quietly, "I wanted you alert, because I want you to know what's happening to you as I kill you."

"No...wha—?" Nhung tried to cry out, but Minh dropped the loop over his neck, then began pulling it tighter. He tightened it very slowly, and although Nhung tried to fight it with his hands, he was too weak and not in a good position to get to it. His face began turning blue, and he let out a gasping death rattle.

"Don't die too quickly," Minh said. A few times he released the pressure, prolonging the death agony for as long as he could. Finally, when his arms grew tired and he grew sick of the game, he squeezed until Nhung's eyes bugged out and all signs of life were gone.

Minh took the belt away, and the body slid down in the cage as far as it could go within the small space. One leg was bent back and up, giving the appearance of a body being stuffed into a trunk. Minh put the belt back on his pants and walked out of the prison feeling that he had, somehow, repaid a debt to Justin.

In the American colony in Saigon official recognition was quickly given to the new provisional government of South Vietnam. The American press published the final casualty list, and announced for the first time that one American, a Lieutenant Colonel named Justin Barclay, was accidently killed by stray machine-gun bullets.

Colonel Barclay [the newspaper said] had spent many years in the Orient and in Vietnam, and was considered by many one of the best-informed experts in Vietnamese affairs. His home of record was the Baptist Home, in Jackson, Mississippi.

The total number of dead on both sides was less than one hundred. All in all, it was a rather bloodless coup, well worth it in the long-run advantage the United States expects to gain.

Antoine Mouchette, who had been reading the American coverage of the coup, put the newspaper down and sat at his table on the patio of the Continental to watch the flow of people on the street just outside. There was very little in the visible layer of Saigon to indicate that a coup had just taken place. The only surface indication was an occasional glance—a quick flick of the eye, really —toward some still-remaining battle scar. But there was the feel of a change, the abstract awareness that life had been forever altered.

A gust of wind, the presage of impending rain, began scattering debris about, and the sidewalk vendors began securing their wares. The many flags along the street snapped and popped in the breeze, and the palm fronds rustled impatiently as the trees bent before the wind.

From somewhere an old poster suddenly appeared, and the face of Diem looked up at Antoine, a ghostly image from the past. It stayed for but a moment, and then was whipped away in one final gust.

The wind stopped, and all of Saigon waited in the stillness before the storm.


THE END

# A LOOK AT RED RIVER REVENGE

## BY ROBERT VAUGAN

The Name is Remington...and he's the best there is. In an untamed territory that grinds most lawmen down to blood and bone, it takes a special breed to make justice more than just a fancy word. A man gunmetal hard, as fast as desert lightning-with the bains to outthink 'em and the guts to out fight 'em. Meet the law west of Stone County-Chief Territorial Marshal Ned Remington.

Remington has his hands full, keeping a beautiful hellfire from the clutches of a killer and visa versa!

*AVAILABLE NOW!*

# ABOUT THE AUTHOR

**Robert Vaughan** sold his first book when he was 19. That was 57 years and nearly 500 books ago. He wrote the novelization for the miniseries *Andersonville*. Vaughan wrote, produced, and appeared in the History Channel documentary *Vietnam Homecoming*. His books have hit the NYT bestseller list seven times. He has won the Spur Award, the PORGIE Award (Best Paperback Original), the Western Fictioneers Lifetime Achievement Award, received the Readwest President's Award for Excellence in Western Fiction, is a member of the American Writers Hall of Fame and is a Pulitzer Prize nominee. Vaughn is also a retired army officer, helicopter pilot with three tours in Vietnam. And received the Distinguished Flying Cross, the Purple Heart, The Bronze Star with three oak leaf clusters, the Air Medal for valor with 35 oak leaf clusters, the Army Commendation Medal, the Meritorious Service Medal, and the Vietnamese Cross of Gallantry.